CASTLE
CAY

LEE HANSON

CASTLE CAY

ROOK

RB

BOOKS

CASTLE CAY
Copyright © 2010 Lee Hanson

Published by Lee Hanson as ROOK BOOKS
The First of **The Julie O'Hara Mystery Series**
Second Revised Edition, August 2012

ISBN: 978-0-9881912-3-5
Library of Congress Cataloging-in-Publication Data

Cover Design by Eli Blyden | www.CrunchTimeGraphics.net

*For Janice Jerome,
my invaluable Reader-in-Chief*

PROLOGUE

H e was naked and slick with sweat, despite the coolness of the room. Moonlight sliced through the partially open verticals, casting a striped pattern of light across his body. The ceiling fan made a low, hypnotic sound and was spinning so fast its blades were invisible. The weighted bottoms of the vertical cloth slats moved silently in the breeze. Within reach on the nightstand, a plethora of prescription drugs stood ready to aid sleep or relieve pain.

Surprisingly, the needle slipped right into the vein on the first try.

If there's a hell, I'm going there...

1

U nlike most Floridians, Julie didn't want to live by the sea. Her condo overlooked Lake Eola Park in Downtown Orlando, fifty miles inland and twenty miles northeast of Disney. It was an older building with only four floors, but Julie had the whole top-right corner with a clear view of the urban lake across the street, which was interesting and pretty…and small enough not to give her bad dreams.

It was just after eight in the morning and the French doors to the balcony in both her bedroom and her living room were flung wide to let in the balmy September air. Julie was in her tee shirt and shorts, lying in the sun on her chaise. She had closed her eyes and knit her hands together on her chest. Her legs were too long for the chair and her narrow, bare feet hung over the cushion.

She had towel-dried her shoulder-length hair, planning to let the sun finish the job while she read the Sunday paper, but she'd become so comfortable that she had let the bulky edition slide to the floor. She was lulled. Breathing deeply, she savored the rain-washed air that brushed her skin like a satin slip and rustled gently - *swish, swish* - through the ancient oaks. A mockingbird sang one soft trill after another.

Julie was pleasantly drifting off when the unmistakable sound of smashing pottery snapped her back. Her eyes popped open.

"Shit, Sol! What did you do now?"

Quickly rising, she scooped up the newspaper, dropped it on the outdoor table and hurried inside. Her living room/library was arranged more for work than leisure, with a large cherry and glass desk sitting in front of a wall of books. Her big Bengal cat lay there, peering over the edge. He had knocked over an oversized coffee mug, which had shattered on the dark hardwood floor and dumped Julie's cache of odd pens and pencils.

Sol was a year old when Julie adopted him directly from his overwhelmed owner. A genetic throwback, the exotic-looking spotted cat was twice the size of a typical housecat and couldn't be let outdoors. Now, for her trouble, he was gleefully crouched on her desk like a leopard cub that had just whacked a rabbit.

"Damn it, Sol. How come I'm not the alpha cat here? How come that only works with dogs?"

Sol sat up to his full height on the desk, dwarfing the computer monitor. He cocked his head, curious at her reaction, as if she were a littermate with very odd priorities.

She was picking up the mess and scolding him when the phone rang. *So much for the Sunday paper...*

She decided that she wasn't going to answer it, but out of curiosity, she checked the caller ID. To her surprise, the call was from Boston, but she didn't recognize the number.

"Hello?"

"Julie? It's Pete. Pete Soldano."

"Pete! My God! It's been years! Are you coming down to Orlando?"

"No, I'm not, Julie, but you might wanna come up here. I guess you didn't see the paper yet?"

"My paper? The newspaper?"

"Julie, it's about Marc Solomon. He's dead. A drug overdose. It's in the paper up here, I don't know if it's in yours."

"That can't be right! I just saw Marc and David, not more than a month ago!"

"I'm sorry, Julie. I'm afraid it's true. Look, why don't you go see if the story's in your paper, then call me back. The funeral's gonna be up here. If you wanna come up, you can stay with Joan and me. We can go together."

Julie was stunned; it took her a full minute to reply. "Okay, Pete. Uh, okay. I'll call you back."

Shaking, she scribbled the number on a pad, and ran out on the balcony. She stood at the table, flipping frantically through the paper. If any birds were singing, she was no longer aware of it.

KEY WEST ARTIST DIES

The art world lost a rising star on September 8th, with the death of Marcus Solomon. The artist's body was discovered early Saturday morning by his companion, David Harris.

Key West Chief of Police Jeffrey Sanders was cautious in responding to reporters' questions about the possibility of a drug overdose. "It's too early to speculate about Mr. Solomon's death. We cannot confirm intentional or accidental death. We'll leave that determination to the medical examiner."

Mr. Solomon was 38 years old...

There was more, mostly biography.

Julie exhaled a cry, grabbed her stomach and fell into the nearest chair as if she'd just taken a punch to the gut.

We were celebrating... We danced at the Sunset Party! Yes, he had AIDS...but he was doing well...

Suicide? There's no way...not Marc!

It had to be an accident!

Oh no, no...

After a time, she managed to compose herself. She called Pete back, and found out that the Solomons hadn't scheduled the wake and funeral; the body hadn't been released to them yet.

The body.

A wave of nausea gripped her, held her.

She managed to tell Pete she was definitely coming up and asked him to please call her as soon as he knew any more. And then she hung up and cried, and cried some more.

When the endless day grew dark, she slept…empty and shattered like the mug that had once held together her pens and pencils.

2

The pain of the previous day had given way to a pervasive, deadening grief that filled every part of Julie's body. Like an automaton, she left her red Honda scooter behind and struck out for her office on foot. Her destination, a two-story vintage house, was less than a mile away on Cypress, a dead-end street on the east side of Lake Eola.

The sky was a robin's egg blue and a light breeze wafted through the giant oaks, lifting their lacy hems of moss. Neighbors, walking a dog or pushing a carriage, smiled at her as they passed. Julie was so numb that none of it registered. It seemed to her that she had just left her building and suddenly found herself facing the lake at the end of Cypress, turning left into the bricked parking area in front of her office. The handsome amber house was angled toward the water, white columns gracing a wide veranda. Only the gold plates on the dark green double door hinted at the business done inside. The left one read, "Garrett

Investigations". The right plate had only one word...
"Merlin".

For the past three years, Julie had leased her office
space from Joe Garrett, a private investigator who lived
upstairs. Her office was on the right and his was on the
left. For a change, she was actually hoping to see him.

At that moment, Joe Garrett came out and started
down the front steps. He was a tall, broad-shouldered
guy in a dark tee shirt and jeans, a little older than Julie,
perhaps forty. He was ex-military, which probably
accounted for his no-nonsense haircut. He smiled when
he looked up and saw her. "Morning, Merlin," he called
out. "You're up bright and early."

As she approached, he saw the desolation on her
face. "What's the matter? You look like your best
friend died."

Julie handed him the paper coldly, folded to show
the article. "He *was* my best friend."

"Oh, Jesus, I'm so sorry, Julie..."

Grief pierced the dullness like a sharp knife. Joe
was one of the few people she knew who called her
"Merlin" one time and "Julie" the next ...just like Marc
had always done.

"Wait a minute," he said, scanning the article. "Is
this the guy you visit down in the Keys?"

"Yes, it is. Marc and his partner, David. I haven't
been able to get David."

"So it just happened Saturday?"

"I guess so," she said, holding back tears. "Joe, I

was thinking about your friend, Jake Goldman, the attorney in the Keys. Do you think he could get some more detail about this?"

"I don't know, but sure, I'll call him." Concerned, he put a hand on her shoulder.

"Good, thank you," she said, moving away.

Joe got the message. "Well, I'll call you later, okay?"

"That'd be good. Thanks a lot. I'll be here most of the day."

Julie turned, quickly climbed the steps and went into her office.

Luz Romero, Julie's assistant, was already at her desk, sipping coffee. She was a tall, well endowed woman in her late forties who was blessed with thick and glossy black hair which she twisted in a chignon at the nape of her neck. Unfortunately, the same Latin genes had given her equally heavy lashes which seemed to pull the outer corners of her lovely brown eyes downward, suggesting a sadness that was rarely the case.

A warm-hearted, single woman who thought of Julie as a daughter, Luz took one look at her boss, and was out from behind her desk. "What happened?" she asked, hugging her close. "Are you all right?"

Julie's face crumpled, despite her resolve. "No, I'm not. My friend died." Julie handed her the paper.

"No," said Luz, incredulous, "your artist-friend?"

"Yes."

Julie grabbed some tissues. After a moment, she regained her composure. "I need to clear my calendar, Luz," she said, heading for her desk in the other room. "I'm going to Boston for the funeral. I'm not sure yet of the dates, but I'll know soon. I'll probably go to Key West, too. Anyway, I need some time for this. Will you bring the schedule in?"

The two of them spent the rest of the morning rearranging her itinerary. Later, when Luz left for lunch, Julie's eyes fell on her business card:

MERLIN

She smiled. *Marc adored my crazy name.* Julie had hated it in the beginning. She was a corporate trainer, a body language expert, not a magician! But the odd single name had been an undeniable boon for her business. She had John Tate, an attorney, to thank for the moniker.

She'd only been a few months into her consulting business when Robert Cronin, an accountant with the Lindsor hotel group - one of her clients - was murdered. His body, shoeless, was found in the dense shrubbery behind the parking lot of their headquarters in Orlando.

The police, following an anonymous tip, had found the shoes in the backseat of a beat-up old Toyota, which belonged to a drug addict who lived nearby.

Julie had never met Cronin but, as it happened, she knew the accused. During a drug-free period, Michael Trudeau had been hired by Lindsor to sell timeshare in

LVC, the new Lindsor Vacation Club. He'd been in a training class Julie was conducting for Lindsor to help their new hires recognize different social styles and deal with them more effectively. Julie had been impressed with the young man's demeanor and the questions he'd asked. She had a hard time believing that Michael Trudeau could kill anyone.

And for what? A pair of shoes?

Julie had offered her services as a body language expert to John Tate, Michael's attorney. She sat at John's side and advised him during jury selection, skillfully helping to ferret out biased and unsympathetic jurors. Most important, she identified two who could be counted on to side with the defense.

The state's case was circumstantial and the jury had acquitted Michael Trudeau. When interviewed later by a local TV reporter, the two jurors' comments had confirmed Julie's analysis.

John had teased her afterwards. "I'm going to call you 'Merlin the Magician'."

"Don't you dare!" said Julie.

And so, of course, he did. When Luz answered the phone, John would ask for "Merlin." He dutifully referred Julie to his colleagues, too, but always as "Merlin." Her reputation and demand as a body language expert had flourished exponentially.

She shook her head, thinking back on it.

There was never any magic, John.

I just see what people aren't saying.

3

"The Solomons got word last night that the Coroner in Key West is gonna release the body for shipment back to Boston," said Pete Soldano. "They're plannin' the wake for Tuesday night, September 18th, with the funeral the next day. Want to come up Monday and stay with us?"

"Sounds fine, Pete, thanks. Tell Joannie I'm looking forward to seeing her. Don't worry about picking me up; I'll rent a car at the airport. See you guys soon."

Julie spent the next few days finishing up some work. Luz, who adored Julie's cat, offered to spend time with Sol twice a day while she was gone.

At last, she was on her way to Boston. The plane was full, but, thankfully, it was quiet up front. Julie felt so bone tired. She wanted nothing more than to lay back and rest. She hadn't been sleeping well at all since Marc's death.

Joe Garrett's friend, Jake Goldman, had told him that the Key West police – unofficially - considered the case a probable suicide. Julie simply couldn't believe that. If only she could talk to David. Surely, he'd be at Marc's funeral.

She closed her eyes as her thoughts drifted back to Marc.

Eighteen years ago.
Such an odd place to meet...

4

June 1989
Boston, Massachusetts

I t's too damn hot for pants!

Julia scolded herself for wearing them as she pulled open the heavy glass showroom door. She sighed with relief as the cool air from inside washed over her. Straightening up, she tucked some stray locks of hair back into the tortoiseshell barrette at the nape of her neck, and looked around.

Five brand-new cars gleamed on the polished floor, and several curious male heads turned her way. Their gaze made her change her mind in a flash. She had gone back and forth over what to wear today; her blue summer dress and heels, or the tan slacks with a plain, white silk shirt and flats. Now, despite the heat, she was glad that she had opted for the latter.

She took a deep breath, squared her shoulders and headed for the circular desk centered on the rear wall. A young, pretty brunette behind the desk looked up at her, smiling.

"Welcome to Solomon Chrysler. May I help you?"

"Yes. I'm Julia Danes. I'm here to see Mr. Soldano."

The girl pulled the big microphone toward her, pushed a button and intoned, "Mr. Soldano. Mr. Soldano. Front desk, please. Customer waiting."

"Oh, I'm not a customer," said Julia. "I'm here for the job interview."

The brunette's brow creased into a puzzled frown. "You must want Mrs. Bennett, the Office Manager?"

"I spoke to a Mr. Soldano on the phone. His name was in the ad…?"

A tanned and dapper, thirty-ish man walked up and interrupted them. "Hi, Julie Danes? I'm Pete Soldano."

He was shorter than she had expected him to be, but then most people seemed short to Julia. They shook hands as he looked her up and down approvingly. Then he nodded to his right.

"My office is just down the hall there." With that, he leaned over the desk, put his left hand over the microphone, and whispered to the receptionist, "Don't put any calls through to my office, Doll. And keep these knuckleheads out here on the floor. I don't want any of them interruptin' me, either."

As they walked back to his office, he smiled broadly at Julia. "So you want to sell cars, huh?" Without waiting for an answer, he turned into a small office with glass windows facing the hallway. "Come on in, Julie," he said, grabbing the chair behind the desk.

She hesitated a moment too long, and then it seemed too late to tell him that her name was "Julia", with an "a".

"Close the door there. Have a seat." He lifted the coffee mug on his desk. "You want some coffee?" he said, as he took his seat behind the cluttered desk and leaned back, making himself comfortable.

"No thank you, sir. I'm fine."

"You know, we used to have a store out in LA with all girls sellin' the cars. They did pretty good. They were all redheads."

Julia had researched the company and knew about them. They all wore the same sexy outfits, too. It didn't last long.

"Really?"

"Yeah, no kiddin'," he said. "So, have you done any sellin', Julie?"

"I've done well selling Avon, sir."

"Avon. That's makeup, isn't it?"

"Yes, sir...but Avon has all kinds of products now. I've been in sales for three years, sir. I'm a group supervisor and I've recruited and trained four girls who work under me."

"How old did you say you are?" he said, skeptical.

"I'm twenty, sir, but I'm really good at sales. I know I could sell cars!"

"Look, Julie, relax. You got the job. And stop callin' me 'sir'."

Suppressing an urge to dance, Julie exited the showroom clutching her "employee paperwork" like a winning bet on a long shot. With a wide, triumphant grin, she jumped into her mother's old Ford, shifted into reverse and backed out of the dealership.

I did it! I got a job with a car. I'll be able to make some real money...I'll be able to move!

Daydreaming all the way home about her future freedom, Julie finally turned into the driveway, lining up the sedan's wheels with the two paved strips in the grass and weeds, as she always did. She pulled up even with the back door to her family's old, white clapboard house. Jumping out, she ran up the crumbling flagstone steps. The wooden screen door banged shut behind her as she absently kicked off her shoes. "Mom, I got the job!" she yelled, stepping out of the hall.

Happiness flew away like a popped balloon.

Julia's mother was kneeling on the kitchen floor. She was crying, her hand bleeding into a puddle of gin, drunkenly trying to pick up the broken pieces of her martini glass. As her mother slowly turned toward her, Julia saw an angry, purple welt on her right cheekbone that was also bleeding.

"Oh, God, Mom! Here, leave the glass," she said, rushing to help her up. "Stop, Mom. I'll get it. *Where is he?*"

"I don' know."

Elizabeth Danes was a mess. Disheveled clothes and crazily teased salt and pepper hair. A sad clown would have envied her makeup.

The usual war of emotions raged within Julia. Her love and pity for her mother had kept her from going away to college, even though she was an honor student. That was three years ago, and it was plainly a mistake. Perhaps this dysfunctional play would close with one less actor, she thought. Or was she the audience? Leaving was the only way to find out.

I can't change things, Mom.
I can't change you.
I can't change him.

Suddenly, the swinging door connecting the kitchen and the dining room burst open, slamming into the side of the stove.

Julia whirled around, every muscle tensed, her fist clenching the glass shards in her hand, not noticing that she'd cut herself.

"What the hell are you doing?" roared her father. "Get away from her! She's a fucking lush! Let her pick up her own goddamn mess!"

George Danes was a drinker who never appeared to be drunk. Over six-feet with silver hair and blue-gray eyes, he could have been cast as a doctor on a daytime soap opera. An avid fisherman and hunter, he was considered a "man's man." Men liked him and foolish women flirted with him. Behind his front door, his wife and daughter feared him.

Not me, Dad. Not anymore.

Julia quickly dropped the broken glass in the wastebasket and grabbed the frying pan off the counter. She stood with her feet planted apart, in front of her cowering mother.

"Stay away from her!" she said, holding up the heavy skillet with both hands.

George stopped in his tracks.

This wasn't the first time she had physically defended her mother. But she wasn't a child anymore, to be swatted away like a pesky insect. She was tall and strong…and she didn't make empty threats.

George smiled and began to laugh.

"Goddamn! At least you've got balls. You take after me."

"I'm *nothing* like you."

"Huh," he snorted.

Still laughing, he turned and pushed through the swinging door to the dining room. Julia heard the front door slam, and the car start up out in front of the house.

She lowered the iron skillet.

"Mom, you've got to get a new bodyguard," she said, wearily. "I'm a car salesman."

5

Pete Soldano phoned Julia the next afternoon to tell her that she needed to be at the dealership the following morning for training. He also mentioned that there would be another person in the class.

At nine sharp, as nervous as a filly in a derby, Julia reported for duty. The store was empty, except for a slim guy with glasses on the other side of the showroom. She walked into the business office behind the reception desk, and found two women. One was standing, cradling a steaming mug of coffee. She had an old-fashioned pageboy hairdo, but appeared to be no more than twenty. Julia gave her a warm smile.

"Hi, I'm Julia...ah, Julie...the new saleswoman. I'm starting today."

"Hi...I'm Annie."

There was no return smile, just a nervous glance at the older woman, who turned toward Julia while pulling out a file drawer.

"Hello, Julie. I'm Mrs. Bennett, the Office Manager. I'll be with you as soon as I tend to a couple of things here. You and Marc Solomon - he's the other person in this class - you need to see some training films. Why don't you go out and introduce yourself to Marc, and I'll come out and get you in a few minutes?"

The showroom seemed cavernous to Julia with the lights off. She made her way around the shiny, new models toward the fellow she'd noticed before. He was sitting at one of the many round tables near the all-glass front of the room, sipping coffee. He saw her coming, and stood up, nearly knocking over his chair.

"Hi, I'm Julie Danes," she said. *That's the new me, Julie.* An overwhelming sense of beginning filled her as they shook hands. "I guess you're Marc Solomon, the other sales trainee?"

"Yup, that's me," he said with a sweet, shy smile. He glanced down and his wavy, light-brown hair fell over one side of his John Lennon glasses. "And, yes," he said, looking up, "I'm related to the boss."

"I thought you probably were."

"My father wants me to learn the business."

The staccato *click-tap* of Mrs. Bennett's pumps echoed through the showroom, and they both turned at the sound.

"Ah, there you are. I see you've found the coffee, Marc."

"Yes…thank you, Mrs. Bennett."

"Please, call me 'Laura', Marc. None of the salesmen call me 'Mrs. Bennett'. Would you like to get some coffee, Julie, before we start? It's right over there, by the Parts department."

Julie hurried to go grab a cup, pondering the word "salesmen".

I don't think I'll call her Laura yet...

6

It was closing time, the end of her second week, and Julie walked to her car as frustrated as a benched ballplayer. Twice that day she had greeted a walk-in, only to find out it was a returning customer who had already met with another salesman. It had been happening to her all week. How could she make a touchdown if she never got the ball?

The very next day, Julie arrived determined to write some business. She was the first one out of the morning meeting...and just in time for the first customer of the day, who was entering the showroom.

"Good morning!" she said, smiling and shaking his hand. "I'm Julie Danes. How can I help you?"

Suddenly, from the back of the room one of the salesman called out, "Hi, John! I'll be right with you!"

Damn...not again!

Julie sighed. "He'll be right out, John. Can I get you some coffee?"

"Sure...but my name's Ted."

Dawn broke over Marblehead.

"I guess he's mistaken you for someone else," she said, taking his arm. "Let's go get that coffee, Ted."

Week three was a bonanza. Julie had three "full-sticker" sales to three happy customers, all walk-ins. She was about to receive the biggest paycheck she'd ever earned, and even though the women in the office still wouldn't give her the time of day, Julie sensed a grudging respect...if not friendship...from the salesmen.

Her mother had called once, sobbing and drunk, carrying on about George. In the past, Julie would have dropped everything and run to her rescue. But she didn't...and life went on. All in all, things were going very well.

That is, until the beginning of week four when Dan O'Hara, the chauvinistic and charismatic New Car Manager, came roaring back from an award trip to Hawaii and crash-landed into Julie's life.

7

September 17, 2007
Boston, Massachusetts

Julie awoke with a start as the plane bounced on the landing strip, amazed that she had slept through the entire three-hour flight. Around her, passengers unclipped their seat belts and opened the overhead bins, but Julie remained seated, concentrating on details long past, reluctant to let go. Despite her effort, most of her dream slipped away.

Eager now to see Pete and Joan, Julie waited impatiently with the crowd exiting the plane, and then made her way quickly through the airport, boarding the bus to Hertz. As she drove along Route 1 North toward their house in Salem, she thought back to the last time she saw Marc and David. She had gone down to Key West to visit them.

It was a celebration, Julie recalled. They had gone with Susan Dwyer, Marc's agent, to Mallory Square for the Sunset Party. Later, they had closed up the Hog's Breath Saloon. Julie focused on their conversation. Marc was getting bombed, she remembered, smiling. He was talkative, exultant...

"I finally did it, didn't I? I'm so excited! Rave reviews in the Globe and the Herald. Did I tell you I sold several big pieces?"

"Yes! I'm so happy for you, Marc."

"You know the best part of it? The show was in Boston, right under their noses."

"Whose noses?" she asked, laughing.

Marc's demeanor suddenly darkened.

"Dear old Dad and Evil Av."

Julie was confused.

"Avram? Your brother?"

Susan interrupted.

"C'mon, Marc. He's not that bad. He makes sure you get your check every month."

Julie was taken aback by Marc's reaction; he flared at Susan.

"It's not from him!"

Susan just sat there, stunned into silence. It was an embarrassing moment.

Marc, drunk as he was, realized he was out of line. He immediately quelled his anger. He waved his hand dismissively.

"Oh, the hell with Av," he said, putting his arm around her. "If we can agree on some stuff, Susan is

going to get me a show in New York!"

Julie couldn't remember talking about Avram again that weekend. Surprisingly, Marc and David had been planning a trip to Castle Cay in the Bahamas. They'd talked about it a lot, but Julie didn't remember one word of that.

Castle Cay.

Did I deliberately tune that part out?

The mere thought of the place literally stopped her cold. She pulled off the road near a quiet intersection and sat there, nauseous.

A cold, familiar sweat crept across the nape of her neck and she shivered. *Why would Marc go to that cursed island?* Julie had trained herself to quickly cut off thoughts of Castle Cay when they surfaced. She struggled to bring herself back to the present.

Pete and Joan. They're waiting for me. Where the hell am I?

She pulled out her cell phone and called the Soldanos. Their house was "ten minutes away"; they told her to "continue on the exit road, north to the river".

Julie kept the river on her left as directed, driving slowly, squinting at each street sign on the right. The area was heavily wooded, and it was growing dark and difficult to see. She didn't want to have to turn around on the narrow, two-lane street, which was edged on the left with nothing more than a tiny rock wall and some birch trees above the riverbank.

At last she saw it, an oval sign on her right, rimmed in gold:

Drake Hill

She turned right up a steep grade and immediately saw their house, ablaze with lights. Like the other five houses on the short street, it was nicely landscaped and set among the large, granite boulders of the hill. They were waiting for her outside. She got out of the car and they all hugged each other warmly.

"Look at you two, you've hardly changed." *They're a matched set*, Julie thought - not for the first time - about her friends who looked more like a brother and sister. Dark haired and a few inches shorter than she, Pete and Joan were fitness fanatics who walked and biked daily. They were beach-lovers, too, and deeply tanned. Julie could see some craggy lines on Pete's face and his hair had thinned some, but not a strand was gray. Julie thought he looked great. And as for Joan…she was as pretty as ever.

"Your house is beautiful. I love the way the homes are built around the boulders. We don't have anything like this in Orlando."

"Yeah, it's nice here. We built the place," said Pete with pride.

"Julie, I made a dinner reservation for eight o'clock," said Joan. "We're going to have to leave *right away* if we want to make it, you know? Pete, why don't you take her bags inside the house."

"No problem," said Julie quickly. "Don't worry about my bag; we can take it in later. Hop in…I'll drive. Where're we going?"

"Pickering Wharf," said Joan.

Pulling into the familiar waterfront area was bittersweet for Julie, who remembered going there with Dan. The three ate in a favorite seafood restaurant, and brought each other up to date on their lives.

Julie talked briefly about Orlando and her business and they laughed when she told them about her cat, Sol, and his independent ways. Pete and Joan beamed with pride as they talked about their boys, Pete, Jr. and Paul.

Julie learned that Solomon Chrysler had grown to three locations, and that Pete was now the GM of the Lynn store. They reminisced about the folks they knew who still worked for the company.

But the tragedy in Key West couldn't be pushed into the background for long. Joan was the one who finally went where no one wanted to go.

"Was Marc terminal, Julie?"

Julie sighed.

"Yes, he was, in the sense that AIDS isn't curable. But was death imminent? No it wasn't, Joan. He looked good when I saw him. He was happy."

"We went to his show on Newbury Street," said Joan. "I loved Marc's paintings… especially the Castle Cay ones, you know?"

Pete interrupted his wife.

"The ol' man, Milton? He didn' go, y'know," he said, fuming. "Can you believe that? He's one stubborn son-of-a-bitch!"

"Pete," shushed Joan, her hand on his arm. "Keep your voice down."

"Sorry. It just gets me mad. Marc never deserved to be treated the way the ol' man treated him. When Miriam died, Milt and Avram both acted like Marc didn' exist."

"Avram did go to the art show, Pete."

"Did you talk to him?" asked Julie.

"No," said Pete, "He was with some dame."

"Maybe Avram's finally ready to settle down," said Joan.

"Yeah, *right*," said Pete.

On that note, he peeled off a tip for the waitress, and they left for home.

The day's measure of grief and travel had taken their toll. Julie sank into the sofa-bed in the guestroom, pulling the blankets up to her neck against the chilly air. She missed Marc terribly and fell asleep remembering another time….

8

December, 1989
Boston, Massachusetts

They were seated at their favorite table in the alcove by the bow window inside Blum's Bakery & Deli, two blocks from the dealership. The windowsill was egalitarian, sporting Hanukah candles and a miniature Christmas tree. Julie looked through the lightly steamed panes at the snow blowing around outside. The little restaurant was renowned for its soups and sandwiches and was filled to capacity with lunchtime regulars, who were as dependable as kids around an ice-cream truck. Julie watched as each of them stamped their wet boots and unconsciously smiled as they entered.

The cacophony of voices actually made for privacy and the two of them found it a cozy spot for conversation. But, for some reason, Marc wasn't his usual chatty self. He had finished his pastrami sandwich in near silence, and now he was studying her with a very serious expression.

"I'm leaving, Julie. I can't sell cars. I haven't had a sale in a month."

"Marc, don't say that…you have to be more positive."

"All right, how's this? I'm *positive* I'm not cut out for this. Seriously, I just can't take it anymore. I can't. I've had it."

"Oh, stop. It's all in the numbers. If you see enough people, someone will buy. Besides, it's not *you* they're rejecting; it's the car, or the deal."

"Why can't they be nice, though?" he whined.

Oh, God, not that again.

"Look…people are defensive in a sales situation, Marc. You have to stop taking it personally."

"I can't help it! Besides, I want to go back to art school. My Dad's going to be pissed, but my mother understands. I'm going to tell Dan today, Julie. Hell, he's expecting it."

Julie slumped in resignation. *It was always just a matter of time.* She could tell that Marc's decision wasn't going to change, no matter what she said.

"Oh, damn. I suppose you're right. But I'm going to miss you so much!"

They were getting up to leave; Julie smiled and poked him in his shoulder.

"Do you realize I'll be eating lunch all by myself, you selfish brat?"

"Oh, I don't know about that," he said, helping her with her coat. "You could invite The Divine Dan to lunch."

Solomon Chrysler's New Car Manager, Dan O'Hara, was six-foot-five with wavy black hair and green eyes. Marc, who had a crush on him, generally referred to him as "Superman" or "The Divine Dan". Julie couldn't stand him.

"*Not* funny. He hates me and the feeling is mutual. I'm going to miss you terribly, Marc," she said as they headed for the door. "Promise that you'll keep in touch with me?"

"Of course I will."

"Solemn promise?"

"Solemn promise."

9

It was eight months since she had come to Solomon Chrysler and although Red and Pete were the only ones in her fan club, Julie was happy. Except for one thing…and it was happening again.

"I have to say, that car's got a real nice ride, Julie," said Mr. Gilbert.

"I just love it, Julie," said Mrs. Gilbert.

Time to turn it over…

Julie deeply resented having to turn over her customer to a "closer". She didn't like subjecting them to that transition. And besides, she was perfectly capable of closing her own sales!

"Excuse me, Mr. and Mrs. Gilbert; I'm glad you've settled on a car you'd like to buy," she said, "but I'm new here…"

How long must I keep saying that?

"So, I'll need to get a manager to help you," she continued. "I'll be right back. Can I freshen up your coffee before I go?"

After topping off their coffee, Julie went looking for Pete or Red - or whoever was available - but everyone was busy. Dan O'Hara looked up as she walked by.

Oh, please, God...not Dan.

"Julie? You need some help? "

Actually, I don't, she thought.

"Uh, yes," she said. "My people are waiting to close. They're interested in a used Imperial, but Pete is with another customer." Brightening, she said, "Why don't I go see how long he'll be?"

"No, don't bother him," said Dan, getting up. "I'll go with you. Where are they?"

Resigned, Julie handed him her worksheet and said, "They're over on the left side of the showroom, in front of the window. The Imperial is parked right outside where they can see it."

"All right. Introduce me," said Dan, straightening his tie. "I'll take it from here."

Oh, thank you, Your Highness, Julie thought as she led him to the table.

"Mr. and Mrs. Gilbert, I'd like to introduce you to Mr. O'Hara, one of our Sales Managers."

"Hi, folks. Call me Dan," he said, smiling. He glanced down at the worksheet. "Is it all right if I call you John and Cecile?"

"Sure," said Mr. Gilbert. He gave a perfunctory nod toward his wife. "You can call the wife 'Cece', though."

"So, John, did you watch the Red Sox game last night?" said Dan, pegging him as the decision-maker.

"Man, that Roger Clemens...isn't he something?" said Mr. Gilbert with a big smile, bonding with Dan.

Cece and Julie were immediately relegated to the bench.

When the Gilberts drove off in their newly acquired Imperial, Dan marched Julie into his office. Closing the door, he turned and glared at her, livid.

"Haven't you learned *anything*?" he barked in her face, throwing the papers down on the desk. "You aren't supposed to talk when I'm closing! Don't you know they need to focus on me? Your talking takes their attention off of me and off the deal!"

"Mrs. Gilbert asked me a question," said Julie through clenched teeth. "I thought it would be rude not to answer her." She probably should have stopped there, but her building resentment just spilled out unchecked. "Besides, you and Mr. Gilbert were completely ignoring her. No *wonder* she started talking to me."

Dan's eyes widened, infuriated at her insubordination. A vein pulsed on the side of his temple and she could feel the anger radiating from him. He was crowding her, so close that she was forced to crane her neck up to look at him but she refused to give him the satisfaction of backing up.

"Look…*Julie*…" he said in her face, "buying a car is a *man's* business. A guy may come in here with his wife, but when he's ready to buy, it's just him and the sales-*man*, another guy in a shirt and tie. It's not his wife's decision!"

"Well, I seem to be doing all right talking to *both* of them!" she shot back.

"Beginner's luck, lady. By the way, did you know you were hired as a *gag*?"

Julie caught her breath and backed away as if he'd slapped her. Her face burning, she grabbed the papers off his desk and fled.

"Why didn't you tell me, Pete? Did everyone know?"

Pete Soldano looked thoroughly distraught across his desk. "No! Nobody knew that but me and him," he said. "I can't believe he told you that. The bastard! Pardon my language."

"Him? He's not the one who hired me as a joke!"

"Look, I'm sorry, Julie. I mean…I'm not sorry that I *hired* you…" Pete ran his hands through his hair in frustration trying to explain. "It's true that in the beginnin' I was tryin' to get back at him for winnin' the trip, and I knew if I hired a girl it would piss him off. I'm *sorry* for that. But, honest-to-God, Julie, I saw you had talent right away and I told him."

If repentance had a picture next to it in the dictionary, Julie thought, it would be Pete. She sighed. *It is a man's game.* Hadn't she been to three other dealers first? And what if Pete hadn't hired her? *I wouldn't be in my apartment...*

"All right. I guess I understand. But, please, Pete, you've got to let me go start to finish with my customers now. You owe me that much and you know I can do it! I promise to turn over anyone I can't close."

"I got no problem with you closin' in *my* department, Julie. But forget Dan. He'll never do it...especially not now."

"Please, Pete. Just get Dan to give it a try for a month. Just *one* month! Tell him I'm really upset. Tell him that I'll probably quit if I fail. *That* should give him some incentive."

"You wouldn't do that, would ya'?" said Pete, alarmed.

"Are you kidding? You couldn't drag me out of here now with the tow truck!"

10

D an O'Hara's attitude lit a fire under Julie. She began closing her own sales and never looked back. By her second anniversary at the dealership, at age twenty-two, Julie was the top salesperson for Chrysler in the state of Massachusetts and the Boston Globe sent a reporter out to interview her. His first question would have a lasting impact on her future.

"So what's the secret of your success?" the reporter asked.

"Body language," said Julie. "I think it's a key element to understanding people and what they want."

"And how do you feel about being the top salesperson for Chrysler in the state?"

Julie saw her chance to win over her co-workers and grabbed it:

"The guys I work with here at Solomon Chrysler are all excellent salesmen. This year was my turn; next year one of them will outsell the rest of us! Plus, we have a terrific service department here, too. Those guys really stand behind the promises we make, and that means a lot of return business. But if it were up to me, I'd give the award to the ladies in the business office. Without them, none of us would sell anything!"

The article said in closing…

"Well, Solomon Chrysler has its very own "Pretty Woman" now, with the addition of young Julie Danes, who, by the way, looks a lot like Julia Roberts. Check it out…"

And lots of curious shoppers did.

Julie's solo lunches were over, and the office manager, Mrs. Bennett, became "Laura".

11

"Are you going tonight? asked Annie. "You know Joannie, from payroll? We're going together. We could meet you there."

"That would be great," said Julie. I'd love to have some company."

They were talking about the company picnic. It was scheduled for the evening of the Fourth of July. Solomon Chrysler had staked out an area along the Charles River near the Band Shell for the Boston Pops outdoor symphony. Julie was excited to be going. It would be the first time for her.

She called Marc and gushed about it.

"I'm psyched! Can you believe that I've never been to the Boston Pops?"

"No", said Marc, "I've gone many times. I love it. My parents are big supporters of the Symphony."

"The only thing my parents support is the liquor store."

"Julie, everybody has problems. You just can't see them. You're not alone."

"I feel alone, though, Marc. I mean, I'm not unhappy at work, but I just don't have anyone close enough to share things with. I really miss you."

"I miss you, too. But I can't say I miss all those tire-kickers."

"Hey, watch it! Those 'tire-kickers' have been pretty good to me."

"I know. I saw the story in the Globe. Congratulations! But I think they should have given you a public relations award for that speech," said Marc, laughing.

"Thank you. It wasn't bad...if I do say so myself. It sure changed things around here for the better. But I still miss *you*. Hey, why don't you come to the picnic?"

"I can't, Julie. I've already made plans. Look, there's someone I want you to meet. Let's go up to Good Harbor Beach in Gloucester next week. What do you say?"

"Okay, call me. I'll see you then."

———

The Fourth of July was a near perfect night for the Pops. A luminous, full moon shone through the leaves of the tall oaks and maples on the Esplanade and the air was balmy. Along the river's edge, a gentle breeze rustled through the willows.

It seemed that everyone had paired off, camped out in folding chairs and on blankets. Annie had asked sheepishly if Julie minded her "sitting with Mike", one of the mechanics, and Julie noted, with some interest, that Joannie DeAngelo from the payroll department was sitting next to Pete Soldano.

Julie didn't mind at all. She was sitting on a long bench with some other employees, absorbed in the wonderful music…soft at times, and then rising and booming in crescendo.

No wonder Marc loves the Pops…

There was a tap on her shoulder. She turned and looked up. To her shock, it was Dan O'Hara.

"Julie, could I talk to you for a minute?"

"Uh, sure", she said. "Have a seat."

"Maybe we could walk a little?"

He seemed nervous. Was he going to fire her? Then, in a flash, she understood. *He wants to apologize… in private.*

"Sure, that would be nice."

They started walking down the path to the left that ran along the river, away from the large crowd at the Band Shell. A couple, holding hands, approached them, heading in the opposite direction, toward the music. They smiled and passed.

Julie was quiet…waiting.

"I just wanted to say that I was wrong, Julie…wrong about you."

What am I supposed to say to that?

"Will you forgive me? I was a jerk."

Now, that's better...

"Of course I forgive you."

"By the way, that was great," he said.

"What was?" asked Julie, puzzled.

"The way you spoke up for everybody at Solomon Chrysler in your interview with the Globe. I know we didn't make it easy for you at the dealership. I was probably the worst of all."

"Probably?"

They burst out laughing, the tentative mood changed completely.

The boats glided by on the river and the crowd thinned and disappeared as they strolled along, talking. Engrossed, they had walked quite a distance from the Band Shell when they found themselves standing before a darkened boathouse. There was a rack of narrow racing sculls to the left of it and a dock behind it.

Dan cocked his head toward the boathouse, smiling.

"We'd have a great view of the fireworks from that dock."

"We sure would," said Julie.

He took her hand and, giggling like kids, they ducked and ran around to the left rear of the boathouse. There was a chain-link fence dipping down into the water.

"I'm game if you are," said Julie.

Dan kicked off his loafers, rolled up his pant legs and stepped into the water. Holding the bottom of her white sundress and sandals in her left hand, Julie followed him in, hanging on to the chain-link with her right.

"Oh shit! It's all mucky!" she said.

"Did you just say 'shit'?"

"Of course. Who do you think I am...Goody No-Shoes?"

They broke-up with laughter again, and made their way around the fence. As Dan grabbed Julie's hand to help her up the riverbank, he put his forefinger to his lips.

"Sh-h-h..."

Snickering quietly, they ran barefoot along the riverbank past the neatly racked racing boats toward the dock. Dan climbed up first and pulled Julie up behind him. To their delight, there were folding beach chairs amidst some boxes and canvas on the wide deck, just a few steps above them. Dan ran up and got two of them.

They sat, hearts still pounding from their escapade, looking down the moonlit river to where the boats were gathered near the Band Shell. After a while, they began to relax, chatting comfortably and listening to the beautiful music drifting toward them.

Dan rose, smiling, and executed a deep, theatrical bow in front of Julie.

"May I have this dance, Miss Scarlet?"

"Why, yes, of course, Mr. Butler."

Laughing, Julie went into his arms.

And everything changed.

They danced slowly, her head on his shoulder, her

arms around his neck, their bodies pressed together, fitting perfectly. Wordlessly, they searched each other's eyes. Dan kissed her, softly…hungrily. The thin straps of her sundress fell from her shoulders. His hand slipped into the top, caressing her breast.

Julie's mind was buzzing. She was swirling in a maelstrom, incapable of coherent thought. Dan's touch created an exquisite sensation pulsing deep inside her body that obliterated everything else. His leg slid between hers and she moved urgently against it.

Then he was leading her up the stairs. He grabbed the canvas there and spread it on the darkened deck. In the next moment, they were standing entwined again, Julie's back against the deck railing.

Dan's big hands were up under her dress, pulling her close. Her head was thrown back and he was kissing her neck. Julie moaned unconsciously, lost in a new and wonderful world…but her daze betrayed her innocence.

Dan pulled himself back, unused to the situation.

"Don't stop," said Julie in a rush of breath. She bent forward, pushing her dress and panties to the floor, her hair cascading over her shoulders as she stepped out of them.

Suddenly, the dark night sky was filled with crackling explosions and a dazzling display of colors. Julie stood, bathed in the golden light, looking up at the sky in awe.

Dan was in awe, too…but he was looking straight ahead.

12

On the way to the beach the following week, Marc introduced Julie to Alan, which explained a lot. She could tell that Marc was anxious about "coming out," but Julie truly didn't care about his sexual orientation. She figured that it was his business, and it had no bearing on their friendship. Well, perhaps it did. There was no doubt in her mind that, somehow, it made Marc a better friend.

The weekend weather was warm and beautiful, part sun, part clouds. Thanks to an erroneous forecast of rain, they had no trouble finding a space to spread out their blanket. It was high tide, and frothy whitecaps dotted the sea here and there like bits of snow after a thaw.

Alan took their drink orders, and went off to the snack bar at the end of the beach, leaving Julie and Marc lying side-by-side on the blanket, enjoying the salty air. Marc sat up, hugging his knees, looking down at Julie.

"Well…what do you think of Alan?"

"Isn't he a little old for you?" she said.

And that was that.

Julie was actually delighted to see Marc relaxed and happy. They talked about his progress at the Art Institute in Brookline.

"It's fabulous, Julie. I'm learning so much. I'm using all different mediums: pastels, oils, watercolors, acrylics, inks…and different surfaces, too. I'm working on a sculpture; it's okay, but drawing and painting, that's what I want to do."

Shielding her eyes from the sun as it emerged from behind a cloud, Julie looked up at him. "How are things with your parents? Any better?"

"Not bad. My mother's okay with the gay thing, but I don't think my Dad knows. I don't think my brother does, either…but he might."

"Your brother?" said Julie, wide-eyed now and sitting up. "You have a *brother?* I can't believe you never told me! How come you never mentioned him?"

"I just don't like to talk about him. We don't get along. *At all*," said Marc. "He's three years older than I am. You'll probably be seeing him at the dealership. He just finished school. He's an accountant."

"Oh, my God, I think I met him. Is his name Avram? Dark hair and eyes, tall, kind of…brooding? "

"That's him. He looks more like my father. I look like my mother."

"He asked me to lunch…"

"Did you go?"

"No. I was too busy at the time," said Julie. She stared at Marc. "I can't believe you're brothers."

"Yeah, sometimes I can't believe it, either."

They sat for a moment, watching some teenage boys riding the breakers while the gulls swooped and squawked overhead.

"Not to get too personal, Marc, but who else knows you're gay?"

"Well, my friends at school and some teachers, and …you'll never guess who else, Jules."

"A sister you didn't tell me about?"

"No. I don't have any other siblings. Give up?"

"Yes."

"The Divine Dan!"

"Really…How did that happen?"

"He just asked me. He's very straightforward, you know. Actually, I like him a lot. He's a terrific guy. Too bad he isn't gay."

Just then Alan came back with their drinks, and Marc quickly changed the subject.

"So, Julie, did you enjoy the Pops Symphony and the fireworks?"

"Oh, yes…especially the fireworks…"

13

~

September 18, 2007
Salem, Massachusetts

"Julie. Wake up, Julie." said Joan.

"Hmm?" Dreaming, Julie tried to orient herself. *It's not Marc; he's gone. It's Joan.*

"I'm sorry to wake you, hon. It's late; you must have needed the sleep. There's a phone call for you. It's Joe Garrett. Here's the phone. I'll be downstairs."

"Thanks, Joan," said Julie, taking the phone and rubbing her eyes. "Joe?"

"Hi, Merlin. Sorry. Guess I'm waking you up. I got the number from Luz...you weren't answering your cell..."

"Oh, that's okay. Did you find out something else?"

"Yes, and no. Jake said the police still think it's a suicide; there was no forced entry into the house. But there's been some artful reporting in the local papers that you may not have seen up there. Jake said that if it became necessary, he'd represent David Harris."

"David? That's ridiculous! He loved Marc!"

"Julie. They found an empty syringe in Marc's hand. Even though the police only found Marc's prints on the needle, there's a lot of speculation about David. Some have gone so far as to suggest a 'mercy' killing. And of course, they've checked the Key West public records about the house. The fact that David has survivorship rights to a mortgage-free, waterfront home worth *two million*...well, that's definitely more grist for the rumor mill."

Julie was wide-awake now.

"That's crazy. David already owned half the house. None of this makes sense, Joe. Marc just didn't seem that sick to me. Not for any of these stupid scenarios."

"I know. It's only sensationalism, Julie. Key West is a small place; the local media are trying to hang on to the spotlight. Jake and I thought you should know, in case the story heats up beyond Florida. And we thought you might see your friend at the funeral..."

Of course. Poor David, thought Julie.

"You're right, Joe. I haven't talked to David yet. Frankly, what you've just told me, what they've suggested, that was the furthest thing from my mind. I can't imagine what David must be feeling...especially if he knows about this."

"Yes. Well, that was one of the reasons I called. How are *you* doing?"

"I'm doing okay, I guess. Thanks for asking. We met up here, Marc and I. Being here is bringing back a lot of memories."

"Well, concentrate on the good things."

I'm trying to, thought Julie.

"Listen, Merlin. You've got my cell number. Call me if you need me, all right?"

"Okay, Joe. Thanks. I will."

They hung up, and Julie sat there for a while, thinking about that. *No. There are other investigators… maybe in the Keys.*

Shaking her head with resolve, she got up and pulled on her jeans and a sweatshirt. She twisted her hair up into a ponytail, brushed her teeth and headed downstairs. Joan was by herself in the kitchen, loading the dishwasher. It was a cozy room, filled with sunshine and the aroma of freshly brewed coffee and bacon.

"Hey, sleepyhead, welcome up! Want some breakfast?"

"Maybe some coffee and toast? Guess I missed everyone this morning."

"Yep. Pete's gone to work, and the boys have gone to school. But that's good. We can catch up on old times."

"Joannie, speaking of that," said Julie, sliding into the breakfast nook, "it's been a long time since I've been up here. I thought I'd go for a drive later. Would you mind if I met you and Pete at the wake?"

"Of course not."

"Good. Thanks," said Julie, accepting the coffee Joan set in front of her.

"So, how do you like being a stay-at-home mom? Do you miss work?"

"Not at all. I haven't worked since Pete got transferred. Frankly, I was glad to get out of there, you know? I just hated working for Avram Solomon when he took over our payroll department."

"Why?"

"Well, we'd expanded to two dealerships at the time. There's three now, of course. But there's only one central payroll department, Julie. It's still at our old place. So, for one thing, my workload had *doubled.* And you know Milton Solomon! He doesn't like to spend 'unnecessary' money, so of course they didn't enlarge our space, or hire extra help. So I was really overwhelmed, you know?

"And then Avram, well, he thinks he's always right, you know? Well, get this… on more than one occasion, we actually had paychecks bouncing! Can you believe that? With all the money the Solomons have?"

"How could that happen?"

"Well, it was just a matter of them putting a reserve into the payroll account. But, no, every month we'd have *just enough.* So if there was an error, even a small one, the checks would bounce, you know? Can you imagine how embarrassing it was for me, as payroll manager? People like Bill and Red that have been there for years, friends of ours, coming in to tell me their checks bounced? Of course, we honored them right away. But, there was just no need for it, you know?"

"Did you talk to Avram about the reserve?"

"Yes, and you know what he said? He said it was 'none of my business' how they handled their money; that my job was 'just to cut the checks'! He did apologize the next day, but it was humiliating, you know? Anyway, Pete got promoted to GM of the Lynn store right after that, and we moved here to Salem. I wasn't going to commute all the way from the North Shore to Boston…especially to work for Avram."

"Marc never got along with Avram. Any idea why?" asked Julie.

"No, I don't. But it sure didn't help for Miriam Solomon to leave everything to Marc and put Avram in charge of it, you know?"

14

The crisp chill of fall in Massachusetts was bracing, a nice change from the long Florida summer. It was good, though, Julie thought, that she had chosen to wear her dark brown pantsuit and turtleneck, rather than the black dress she'd brought specifically for the occasion.

The park was filled with colorful elms and maples, accented by paper-white birch trees. Some of the dried leaves had already fallen to the ground, and they crunched beneath her boots as she walked along the single-lane road. She knew the pond was just around the curve up ahead.

The wooden bench was still there, in the clearing overlooking the water. Some Canadian geese swam in a V-formation on the pond, sending ripples across the surface.

Julie sat down on the bench.

Now what?

Memories came flooding back.

They were unstoppable, like her tears.

15

July 11, 1992
Boston, Massachusetts

Dan slid the ring on Julie's finger.

"I, Daniel Patrick O'Hara, take this woman, Julia Danes, to be my wedded wife, to have and to hold from this day forward, for better or for worse, in sickness and in health, until death do us part."

He turned his head toward Julie then, and it was her turn.

Julie's eyes never left Dan's face as she made her vow.

"I, Julia Danes, take this man, Daniel Patrick O'Hara, to be my wedded husband, to have and to hold, from this day forward, for better or for worse, in sickness and in health, until death do us part."

They held hands tightly.

"In the eyes of God, and before this congregation," intoned the minister, "with the power invested in me by the state of Massachusetts, I now pronounce you, Daniel and Julia O'Hara, man and wife."

The bride and groom kissed for longer than they should have, while the little church exploded with clapping and cheers.

They had already bought a home and a sunset reception was held there. A dance floor was set up in the center of the rear lawn while a live trio played on the deck attached to the house. Patio tables with floral centerpieces surrounded the pool, and candles in lily pads floated on the surface of the water.

Julie's parents were there and they seemed genuinely happy and proud. To her relief, they didn't over-indulge. Dan's Dad, a tenor, sang at every available opportunity, and Julie was forced to admit to herself– with not a little guilt about her *own* mother – that she simply adored her new Irish mother-in-law.

The rest of Dan's extended clan attended as well: grandparents, in-laws, aunts and uncles, nieces and nephews. It was a bit overwhelming for Julie, coming from a family of three, but she was sure she'd get them all sorted out, sooner or later.

The real treat was when Julie saw her friends from Solomon Chrysler…Milt and Miriam Solomon with Avram and Marc, Laura Bennett, Annie Tiegs, Joannie DeAngeles and Pete Soldano.

"You look beautiful, Julie," said Pete. "We miss you at the store."

"Oh, I miss you guys, too. But I'm really enjoying school. Dan was right about that."

"I went to Boston College, Julie," said Joan. "It's a huge campus. Do you like it?"

"I do. I'm certainly getting plenty of exercise walking from class to class. "

"What's your major?"

"Psychology. I'm not sure what I want to do with it. Right now, I mostly use it to figure out Dan," she said with a laugh.

"Oh, yeah, *right*," said Dan. "She had my number the day she met me!"

Julie was glad they had a few days to recover before flying to the Caribbean. Still, she was excitedly looking forward to their honeymoon.

Castle Cay, their destination, was an outer island in the Abacos chain, a group of cays - or "keys", as Marc pronounced it - in the Northeast Bahamas. The island was privately owned by the Solomon family, who had made the whole trip a fabulous wedding gift.

Marc had raved about Castle Cay:

"You'll love it, Julie. It's so beautiful! It's wild and rugged on the Atlantic side and so lush and different where our house is, on the Caribbean side. That's where our caretaker's farm is, too. The water's not deep at all there and it's as clear as your swimming pool.

"And it's completely private," Marc added, winking. "There couldn't be a better place for a honeymoon!"

16

J ulie and Dan flew from Boston to Miami, where they changed planes for Treasure Cay in the Abacos. It was just a short flight from Miami; it seemed that they no sooner had gotten on the small plane, than they were getting off. The passengers descended an open staircase, swept by the warm Bahama breeze.

"Oh, Dan, look! Look at the palms!"

The tall trees swayed gracefully, swishing in the gentle trade winds like exotic dancers, filling Julie with wonder.

"Boy, it sure is warm," said Dan. "It reminds me of Hawaii, only flatter."

"It'll be cooler on the water, honey," said Julie. "Marc said to take a taxi to the Ferry dock."

They still had quite a way to go to get to Castle Cay. First, they had to board the ferry to Green Turtle Cay, where they were to meet John Drum, the Solomon's caretaker. Mr. Drum would be aboard the

Solomons' boat, *Wave Dancer*, which would take them to the island.

Once aboard the ferry, Dan became as excited as Julie. He'd brought his camera and was snapping pictures, one after the other. "This is great! What an adventure, huh?"

"Yes. I can't wait to see the island!'

They had no trouble finding the Solomon's slip at Green Turtle Cay. *Wave Dancer* was an impressive craft in pristine condition. It was obvious from the equipment on board that the beautiful boat was mostly used for fishing. There was a short, dark haired man on the deck. He had a wiry look about him and a ruddy, weathered face.

"Hello! Are you John Drum?" said Dan.

"Yessir," the man said, smiling. "You must be Mr. and Mrs. O'Hara?"

"Yes, we are." Dan said, as they climbed aboard. "Please, call us Dan and Julie. Thank you for meeting us! Should we call you John?"

"Yessir. That'll be fine, sir...ma'am".

Although he seemed quite friendly, he was plainly uncomfortable calling them "Dan" and "Julie". Just then, a dark-haired teenage boy climbed onto the boat with his arms full of groceries.

"This here's my boy, Alfred."

"Hi," Julie said. "I'm Mrs. O'Hara...or Julie, if you like. This is my husband, Dan. Do we call you Alfred, or Al?"

"Al's fine, ma'am."

John Drum stowed their bags, and directed them to some blue padded seats in the rear of the boat. "There's a cooler right there, if you want a Coke. My missus made some sandwiches; thought you might be hungry. Takes about forty-five minutes to get to Castle Cay. The sea's calm today, so I figured you might want to sit back here...but go ahead inside, if you want. Call Alfred if you need anything. I'll be topside, and I might not hear you. Welcome aboard, and enjoy the trip!"

17

As Julie and Dan approached the western shore of Castle Cay, the first thing they noticed was a high ridge of limestone rock that bisected the island from north to south like a spine. They could see a small wooden building on the beach facing them, and a long dock reaching out, welcoming *Wave Dancer*.

There was a road behind the little building that went to the left and disappeared from sight. To the right, the road led to a large house. It sat back into the lush greenery, about halfway up the hill, nestled right up against the ridge. Directly in front of the house, down the hillside, was the prettiest beach Julie had ever seen, ringed all around with coconut palms.

John Drum explained to them that his farm was at the other end of the road around to the left. He also said that the two houses had their own large generators for electricity, and that each had fresh running water.

"We have a jeep, if you want to use it, but this here's the only road, and it don't go far...just between the houses," he said. "There's paths going around and up over the ridge to the other side of the island. We got three horses, and that's how we usually get around. You're welcome to borrow 'em."

Once the boat was secured, they piled into the jeep and John drove them to the ridge house. After unloading their luggage and groceries, he headed for the door.

"Well, I'll leave you to your unpacking. We'd sure like to have you over to dinner tomorrow night...if you'd like to come?"

"Oh, we'd love to!" Julie said, catching Dan's eye.

"Good enough, then. I'll be by to pick you up at six o'clock. Good night."

They wandered around, from one room to the next. The house appeared to be constructed of heavy wood, save for the stone fireplace in the living room. The floors were a darker type of wood, covered with large, tightly woven mats. Big, colorful cushions graced oversized rattan furniture. Ceiling fans hung from a high roof, which rose on solid beams to a point in the center of the house. Outside, the roof extended well beyond the house in the front and on the sides, and covered a wide veranda.

They stood there, overlooking the beach, gazing out to the sea.

"Julie, this is so beautiful. I don't think I'm going to want to leave."

"Me, either," said Julie, putting her arms around his neck, reaching up into his dark, curly hair. She kissed him, and said, "Let's go try out the bedroom."

The master bedroom was to the right of the living room on the corner of the house. It was a large room with triple sliding-glass doors on both sides opening onto the veranda. On the inside of the doors were white louvered panels, folded all the way to the sides, accordion-style. A telescope on a tripod stood positioned to watch the panorama of sea and sky.

They slid back the glass doors all the way to let in the balmy trade winds, and flopped on the big white bed. Despite their best intentions, in minutes they were sound asleep, lulled by the *whoosh, whoosh,* of the sea.

18

⌒

The morning sky was just beginning to lighten when Dan woke up. He thought he should probably slip out of bed and go make coffee. He looked over at Julie, sleeping soundly, still wearing her shorts and tee shirt. Her thick brown hair, coppery from the summer sun, fanned out across the pillow on the left, her right hand resting, palm-up on the pillow over her head.

She looked so open and vulnerable. Dan was becoming aroused, but he knew that if he attempted to pull off her shorts, he'd wake her up. He wanted to make love to her while she slept, to wake her *that* way. His near continuous desire for his new wife amazed him, and he was no sexual novice! That Julie was a virgin that first night in the boathouse was an important component of it, he knew. Dan had been with many women, but he had never experienced this sense of *possession*. Julie wasn't merely married to him…she was *his*. She belonged to Dan alone, now and forever.

He felt himself getting harder.

Damn. I should go make the coffee.

As he watched her, her eyes slowly opened. She sighed and stretched like a cat. She reached out to touch him.

"Morning… hm-m…I love you…"

To hell with the coffee.

Dan covered her body with his, nuzzling her neck. He tugged at her tee shirt, and she started to help him.

"No, let me do it. Everything…"

He pulled the soft jersey material up and off. She laid there, arms up over her head, exposed and waiting. Her breasts were flattened and her chest was flushed pink. Dan circled a dark brown nipple with his tongue until it stood up straight. She quivered, but she kept her arms loose on the pillow above her head, her eyes nearly closed, knowing that was what he wanted.

Dan knew how impossible it was for her to stay motionless. He loved that he was driving her crazy, and himself, too. He pulled her shorts and silken panties down, off. She was going to move, but he looked up at her…and she stopped.

"Honey, I should shower …"

"No. No shower," he murmured.

"Don't move, Julie… don't move."

19

~

"C'mon, let's go swim!" said Dan.

"Are you kidding?" Julie's legs felt too weak to stand. She couldn't imagine how he had the energy to bound out of bed like that after such rigorous sex.

"Okay, just lay there for a little bit. I'll make the coffee...if I can find everything. We can take it out on the porch, and go swimming afterwards. How's that?"

A fleeting thought of Marc calling him "The Divine Dan" made her smile.

"That sounds absolutely perfect."

Dan made the coffee and was delighted to find a box of glazed doughnuts. They sat on the porch in their underwear, sipping the hot coffee and listening to the birds, their calls so different from the birds at home.

"It sounds like a jungle here," said Julie. "I wonder if there are any jungle-type animals around."

"You mean, besides me?"

"You aren't an animal. You're more like... Tarzan."

Dan lowered his voice and moved his hand up her leg, a leer on his face. "That's us: 'Me Tarzan, you Jane'…"

"Oh, no, you don't, Tarzan. It's too soon!" said Julie, sprinting down the stairs, onto the path that led to the beach. When she reached the shore, she ran directly into the water, with Dan right on her heels. He tackled her and they rolled around for a while like two playful otters.

"Race you!" said Dan.

They took off, swimming straight out.

"Look," said Dan, when they were quite far out. "I can still stand!"

Dan was up to his neck, but the water was over Julie's head, so she hopped into his arms.

"Marc was right. It's like a giant salt water swimming pool," she said, "and we have it all to ourselves."

The beach was a wide, sandy shelf that extended out into the sea. Where they stood, the water was as clear as drinking water, but where the water deepened, the color changed from a light aqua to sapphire blue or emerald. A school of small fish swam in front of them.

"Oh, look! Look!" said Julie.

"Don't move," said Dan.

"Oh, you want to play that game again?" laughing, she reaching for him under the water. "This time it's *your* turn."

"That works for me," he said. "But, first, how about some of that fancy swimming you do at the Y? You've got plenty of room here."

Julie had always loved swimming. She had joined the BC Swimming and Dive team her first year at college, but it had taken too much time away from her studies.

Dan was referring to the synchronized swimming team that Julie had recently joined at the local YMCA. They were fortunate to have a pool at home where she practiced, but it was small.

"Oh, you're right," she said. "But I want to go out where it's deeper. Why don't you go out on the dock? You'll be able to watch me better from there. I'll swim over."

Dan trotted down the beach and out onto the wooden pier.

She was already there by the time he got to the end. He parked himself on the edge of the platform with his long legs dangling, and she started her routine. With so much room and the added buoyancy of the salt water, Julie was sculling and happily inventing new maneuvers beyond the usual spikes and wheels. She swam with the ease of a mermaid, losing herself in the activity.

Suddenly there was a splash, and Dan was in the water next to her.

"Quick! Back toward the house…it's Drum!"

It took Julie a minute to remember that they were in their underwear.

They swam the distance back in record time. Breathless and laughing, they watched John Drum as he got out of his jeep, walked out on the long dock, started up the boat and pulled away. It seemed he hadn't noticed them; or maybe he'd just done a good job of pretending he didn't see them.

Confident that there wouldn't be any more interruptions, they stripped off their wet underwear and settled into a serious game of "Don't move" on the beach.

That evening they met John's wife, Mary, who had killed and roasted a large chicken in their honor. Julie was glad they were only around for the latter part of that process. Mary Drum was a short, friendly woman, every bit as weathered-looking as her husband. She had a disconcerting habit of talking out loud to herself. *Not surprising,* thought Julie, *considering she's the only woman here.*

Alfred entertained them with stories about the island's pirate history. He said that the high central ridge hid one side of the island from the other so well, that the infamous Blackbeard was rumored to have used Castle Cay as a hideout and point of ambush for unsuspecting traders.

After dinner, they walked about the small farm. In addition to an extensive garden, the Drums had a cow and chickens, a dog, and several cats. They also had three horses, and John Drum asked if they were experienced riders. Julie and Dan had both ridden before, and John offered to pick them up again in the morning so they could borrow "Chinaman" and "Daisy" to tour the island.

Later that night in bed, Dan turned to Julie, propped up on his elbow. "I found some snorkeling equipment. Al told me that the reef we saw today is a great place to snorkel. Maybe we'll find some pirate treasure."

"You mean some that Al hasn't already found?" said Julie, laughing. "Wait a minute... what if there's one of those moray eels in there that jump out at you with all those teeth?"

At this, Dan got up on his knees and flapped his elbows like a bird.

"*Chic-ken...Chic-ken...*"

"You fool. Come here and kiss me."

"Ah, she wants to play 'Don't move'."

"Maybe I have a *new* game."

20

There was no doubt that the horses knew where they were going, and Chinaman, Dan's huge black mount, was determined to be first. He took over the lead early on, roughly nudging Julie's smaller, roan horse out of the way. Daisy dropped back agreeably, apparently used to the order.

Julie had packed a lunch and the camera, and she was excited about exploring the island. The uphill path they traveled was narrow, stony, and well used. After a short ride, they could see the ocean ahead of them.

"Julie! Look! It's the Atlantic!"

"Really, Sherlock?"

"Really, Watson," said Dan, with a laugh.

To their disappointment, the trail veered to the right shortly after that, nowhere near the water, which was still some distance ahead behind a densely forested area of cedar and pine. They kept on, knowing that their descending path would eventually converge with the coastline. Finally, the ocean vista opened before them… a vast expanse of deep, cobalt blue.

Julie pulled Daisy up beside Dan.

"Oh, honey, it's so beautiful!" she said.

"Yes, it is. Get a picture."

And so she did.

Her second picture – one that she would treasure forever – was a wonderful shot of Dan mounted on Chinaman. Julie snapped the third picture…to no avail. Dan had been snapping photos ever since the ferry to Green Turtle Cay, so Julie wasn't surprised that the roll had run out.

"That was the last one, Dan."

"There's more film in the case there, Julie.

She found it and reloaded the camera. Testing it, she looked around and took a couple more shots…a picture of the coconut palms near the shore, swaying like graceful showgirls with high-plumed headdresses, and another picture of the tall long-needled pines that all leaned away from the sea.

They led the horses to a low hanging branch and looped their reins around it.

"Let's explore," said Dan, "we can get some more pictures before we eat."

They set off southward, walking along the natural path, which was actually a long limestone terrace. There was a narrow white beach just below them on their left. Dan hopped down the rocks to take a picture.

"The coast goes on and on!" he yelled from below. "The island's bigger than I thought!" He picked his way back up and they continued south on the path.

On their right, as they walked along, they noticed the massive central ridge of the island rising to its highest point. They had circled north of the widest part of Castle Cay and surmised that their beach house must be right behind the imposing tor. On this side, the big ridge was all rock, with a few hardy scrub bushes pushing up through the crags.

"This side gets more of a beating from the weather," said Dan.

"No kidding, Sherlock?"

The next thing Julie knew, she was on her back in the grass with Dan on top of her, pinning her arms.

"You're a wiseass, you know that?" he said, kissing her.

Julie wriggled free, snatched the camera and ran back toward the horses.

"Ha! You forgot to say 'Don't move!'"

She caught Dan on film once again, charging up behind her.

They slowed to a walk and headed northward along the terrace passing the loosely tethered horses, happily chomping grass next to the tall pine. Walking on, they came to a small promontory, with what appeared to be a notch in the rocks at the end. The seawater was crashing in there and shooting up into the air, geyser-like, before rushing back out to sea.

"I've got to get picture of that," said Dan, taking the camera from her, and walking out onto the little point of land.

I hope he's not going to climb down there, thought Julie. "Dan, be careful! Marc said it was rough on this side!"

"I'm not going in the water, Babe," he called back, shaking his head.

Hanging on the rocks and carefully working his way down, Dan descended toward the notch on the left side of the point. Soon, he was out of sight.

Julie was sitting on the edge of the limestone terrace, inexplicably tense. Her legs dangled over the side and she leaned forward and to the left, straining to see Dan. When he appeared again, her shoulders loosened and she started breathing once more.

He walked back toward her.

"Julie…I didn't want to yell from there. It's a little cave, and the ceiling is covered with *bats.* Tiny ones. At first I thought they were birds!" he said, laughing. "I'm going to try to get a picture of them. Don't be alarmed if they come flying out when the flash goes off."

"Okay. Be careful."

"Don't worry. I'm just getting a picture of them. They're harmless."

Then he headed back down.

In a minute, he was out of her sight again.

She heard something…

What was that? Was that Dan?

Julie ran out onto the point and scrambled down the rocks.

"DAN! YOU OKAY?" she yelled into the darkness.

Startled, the bats flew out of the cave en masse, a dark, beating cloud. They engulfed her, squealing. Swatting at her hair, Julie screamed and screamed as she knocked one loose that was caught. Gasping, she hung onto the rocks, petrified.

Suddenly, the water blew up and out of the cave, knocking her down. As she was catching her breath and shaking wet hair from her eyes, a huge swell came rushing out of the mouth of the cave. Dan was face down, like a body surfer, on top of it.

In moments, he went under and came up again...way out, and moving fast.

"DAN! DAN!"

No time! Go now...NOW...while the water's receding...

Quickly, Julie kicked off her shoes and climbed over to a jagged rock, which stuck out further than the rest. She bent her knees and pushed off, diving as far out into the water as she could... praying to God that she would clear the rocks below.

The water was shockingly cold, and the current incredibly fast. There was no undertow; it was moving Julie near the surface, faster than she could swim...faster than anyone could swim! Julie held her breath, tucked her head, and stretched out like a torpedo.

I can get him… I can get him!

When her lungs were empty and aching for air, she surfaced, still being carried by the current, but sensing it had weakened some. Gulping air, she looked around in panic. Oh, God, where was he? Then she saw him ahead of her, rising on the crest of a wave.

NO! He's further! Swim harder…

Julie took a deep breath, tucked her face into the water and swam furiously ahead. Left, right, left, right…she powered through the sea, propelled even faster by the rip current. At last she lifted her head, gasping, and saw Dan in front of her.

"DAN! DAN!" she yelled, reaching him, grabbing at his clothes.

He was unresponsive, unconscious.

It doesn't matter…Swim!

Struggling to keep Dan with her as the current swept them along, Julie managed to get him on his back and hook her left arm under his chin. Holding his head up out of the water, she began swimming with her right arm. She swam in the direction of the current, but fought to make headway to her right. The rip current, though lessened, continued to drag them out to sea.

Julie kicked furiously, her right arm pulling hard, fighting with all her might to get parallel with the shoreline. Fear pumped adrenalin through her body, giving her strength she could never have imagined. Something large brushed against her, but Julie was struggling for their lives, and whatever it was, it barely registered.

She felt the terrible pull fade. Somehow, she had managed the turn; they were free of the damned current!

"We're out of it, Dan! We're out!"

Julie continued to swim parallel to the shore to get as far away from the deadly rip as possible. Almost at the end of her endurance, she turned toward the beach for the long swim back in. She talked to Dan steadily, encouraging him. She thanked God out loud for saving them…and she prayed from the depth of her soul that He would help her make it to the breakers that would carry them in.

Al Drum was working in the garden when Chinaman and Daisy came galloping into the yard, stopping short of their own accord, reins trailing on the ground. Al's mother was hanging sheets on a clothesline.

"Jesus, Mary and Joseph!" she said, dropping the sheet into the basket and running for the barn, as Al went for the lathered, panting horses.

"JOHN! Come quickly! Something's happened to the O'Haras!"

John Drum had been in the barn fixing a heavy deep-sea fishing reel and line. He'd heard the horses come thundering in, and was already on his way out.

"What the hell…?"

He took one look at the horses, and knew something terrible had happened.

"Mary," he said, "you take care of Daisy and Chinaman. Al and me had better take the jeep and find them."

"Can the jeep make it through to the other side on the trail?" she asked, worried.

"It's going to have to, woman! We can't use those horses!"

Mary took the reins from her son, and watched the pair jump into the jeep and gun it, heading east.

It was a difficult and jarring drive, bumping over stones, lurching in and out of ruts. The jeep barely scraped through the areas where horses trod single-file. Branches whacked the windshield. At one point, where a horse and rider had to climb over a small rise, they had to put their backs to the jeep and push it over. Silently, expecting the worst, they searched the trail all along for any sign of Dan and Julie O'Hara. At length, they made it to the wide, limestone-terraced path that ran above the beach. Al was still driving.

"Head south," said John. "If we don't find them, we'll come back and drive north as far as we can."

They hadn't gone far when they spotted them. "Look!" said Al, pointing. "There they are, up ahead on the beach!"

They pulled up and jumped out of the jeep, scrambling down the rocks to the sand where Julie and

Dan lay side by side, face down, half in the water.

They rolled Dan over.

"He's dead," said John, immediately turning his attention to Julie. "She's alive! She's breathing... unconscious. Help me get her up, Al."

"Mrs. O'Hara! Julie! Can you hear me? Julie?" said John.

Her eyes fluttered open slightly.

"Dan? Is Dan okay?"

"It's going to be all right, Mrs. O'Hara. We've got you now," said John.

Mercifully, Julie slipped away before he had to answer.

21

September 18, 2007
Boston, Massachusetts

In Woodland Memorial Park, Julie sat with her face in her hands, crying. I'm sorry, Dan. I'm so sorry! Wiping her eyes with tissues, she rose and slowly walked a few steps over to a simple, flat marker, unobtrusively lined up with others under the trees.

DANIEL PATRICK O'HARA

Julie stood for a moment, then turned and hurried away, fumbling in her bag for the rental car key. Still dabbing at her eyes, she climbed into the Malibu and left the cemetery.

It was difficult to drive, hard to collect herself. Thankfully, she remembered a restaurant she'd passed on her way there. She pulled into a slot in front of it, relieved to see that the lunch crowd had apparently gone.

Julie went directly to the restroom and splashed some cold water on her face. She reapplied her lipstick and patted a bit of makeup under her eyes. Feeling more presentable, she bought a large coffee and a USA Today paper, and looked around for a booth with some privacy.

Her intention had been to distract herself with the newspaper, but the past had hold of her heart and it wouldn't let go. The printed page blurred before Julie's eyes as she recalled her zombie-like mental state after Dan's death. It had persisted for months and very nearly destroyed her.

At the inquest, the Bahamian coroner had said:

"Daniel O'Hara accidentally drowned after suffering a head injury consistent with a fall, thought to have been caused by a slip on the guano-covered rocks in the cave he was exploring."

But Julie knew different. She didn't get to Dan fast enough to save him. The guilt she felt made it impossible to face people, to accept sympathy. She had run away.

Money had not been an issue. She was the beneficiary on Dan's life insurance policy and it was a sizeable amount. When fall came, she had enrolled at the University of Florida in Gainesville.

Julie hadn't made new friends; she didn't want any. Because of Marc Solomon's unwavering loyalty and persistence, Julie had maintained a half-hearted relationship with him, mostly by phone.

But fate had a nasty surprise for her friend, Marc. The summer after Julie had moved to Florida, Marc's mother died of a heart attack on Castle Cay. Marc, who was alone with her when it happened, was devastated. It was John Drum, Julie recalled, who coordinated efforts with Milton Solomon to have Miriam's body taken back to Boston, not Marc.

Deep in denial, Marc had refused to attend the funeral. Julie had understood. She knew that Marc had long felt rejected by both his father and his brother. For him, losing Miriam was like losing his entire family. He had stayed, instead, on Castle Cay. For three weeks, Marc painted through his grief. And when he left there, it was forever.

Julie took another sip of her coffee, thinking back to 1994.

In the months that followed Miriam's death, Marc had returned to school in Brookline, more passionate about his art than ever. For Julie, however, the time had dragged by…interminable, unbearable. She could see little reason to continue on…with anything.

During a break in their schedules, Marc had come to Gainesville to visit her. Julie had been withdrawn, quiet. In truth, there was only one thing she longed to say to him…*Goodbye.*

Marc had guessed what she was thinking:

"Suicide is selfish, Julie! Would Dan have ever done something like that? Would he have left you like that?"

"No...but he's gone."

"Well, I'm not!" said Marc, tears filling his eyes. "It would break my heart, Julie. Promise me, right now, that you won't ever do that!"

She couldn't bear the frightened look on his face. She hugged him tightly to her. "It's all right, Marc. I won't. I promise."

"Solemn promise?"

"Solemn promise."

Julie stood and put a tip on the table, leaving her unfinished coffee and paper behind. She was ready for Marc's wake now.

22

Skirting limo drivers and furtive smokers, Julie climbed the stairs of the stately Woodland Memorial Funeral Home. She found Marc's room, the main salon. It was filled to capacity with roses and mourners.

Pete and Joan were already there. They were standing with a small group, talking quietly. Julie signed the guest book, and nodded to them, indicating that she was going to see Marc. On her way to the casket through the center of the room, she noticed the Solomons were seated on the left, near the front. She would go there, afterward.

It wasn't as horrifying as Julie had feared. The lifeless body didn't look like Marc. In truth, it *wasn't* him. Marc was in God's hands now. Julie closed her eyes and knelt beside the coffin. Tears welled, but quickly dissipated, as intense anger trumped grief. At that moment, Julie made her last and most solemn promise to her friend.

I know you didn't do this, Marc. I won't let them say you did, my dear friend. Someone else did this...and I'm going to find them. I'm going to make them pay.

Julie rose, and walked over to the family. Marc's brother, Avram, rose to greet her. He was darkly handsome and taller than she'd remembered.

"Avram, I'm so sorry about Marc."

"Julie. Thank you for coming all the way from Florida," he said, holding her hand in both of his. "That was nice of you. It would have meant a lot to Marc."

Nice of me? Surely he knows how close we were? And he's holding my hand in both of his, a politician's grip.

"I can't believe it," she said, "I was just down to see them. Marc mentioned that he'd been talking with you recently?"

"Yes...just some business matters...on the phone".

He hesitated and added the bit about the phone; the corners of his mouth are drawn down, too, a negative expression.

"He looked well to me, Avram. How was he when you talked to him?"

"He seemed fine, Julie." He brushed some hair off his brow. "I guess that's why this whole thing has been such a terrible blow."

He touched his forehead. He's looking in my eyes, but not blinking. His face doesn't match his words. For whatever reason, he's lying.

"Yes. An awful shock," she said.

It was obvious to Julie that Avram wasn't grieving. Of course, there was a simple explanation for that. He and Marc didn't get along. Avram could simply be happy to be rid of Marc. It would be natural for him to try to hide that in this circumstance.

Is that what I'm picking up? But the handshake was an over-the-top attempt to appear genuine. I'd like to know if he visited Key West recently.

She moved along the reception line to Marc's father, who was seated next to Avram. The man was a shell of himself, no longer recognizable as the dominant person who had once been her employer.

"Hello, Milton," she said, shaking his hand. "You may not remember me; I'm Julie O'Hara. I used to work at the dealership. Marc was a dear friend. I'm very sorry for your loss."

"Hello, Julie," he said. "Of course I remember you. I went to your wedding." A deep melancholy overtook him. "Marc never got married; he never had children."

Her heart went out to him in his grief, and she attempted to cheer him with a positive thought.

"There are a lot of young people here. Are they nieces and nephews?"

"They're all Castles, not Solomons. Unless Avram gets married, there won't be any more Solomons."

"Castles?"

"Miriam's family," he said.

"Oh. Yes, of course."

Julie didn't recall Marc ever mentioning his mother's maiden name. Suddenly, Castle Cay came to mind and she realized that it must have belonged to Miriam. She had always thought the name came from the towering ridge.

Who owns it now? Did she leave it to Marc?

Giving the old man's hand a gentle squeeze, she said. "Take care, Milton."

Julie turned and crossed the room to join Pete and Joan. "Hi. Have either of you seen David Harris?"

"I just met him, Julie. He's over there," said Pete, nodding to an area not far from them.

It was easy to spot David with his collar-length light blond hair. He had the same slim build as Mark. As usual, he was dressed perfectly for the occasion. He was standing in a group with Susan Dwyer, Marc's agent and co-owner of the Sandpiper Gallery in Key West. Julie asked the Soldanos to excuse her and went over to see him.

David saw her approaching. He turned and came toward her with his arms outstretched. His eyes were red, his face streaked with tears.

"Oh, Julie, what am I going to do? How can I live without him?"

She hugged him tightly, tears coming to her own eyes. "I'm so sorry, David. I don't know what to say; I hate that he's gone, too."

"I know it was hard for him to bear sometimes," said David, "but he said he'd learned to live with it."

Julie knew he was speaking of Marc's illness, AIDS, the specter of which threatened all the gay community, including David, himself. Nevertheless, as much empathy as she had for him, Julie remembered her promise to Marc.

"I tried to call you several times, David."

"I'm sorry, Julie. I couldn't handle all the press and the crank calls; I just stopped answering the phone. I didn't even check the messages after awhile."

"You were together the night before?"

"Yes, we had dinner with friends, Susan and Rolly. They left around ten-thirty."

"How was Marc that night?"

"He was fine, just tired. After they went home, we said goodnight and he went to his room. You know we have our own rooms now."

Julie noticed that David had momentarily slipped into the present tense, as grieving people often do.

"I never got up during the night," he said. "I usually do, but we finished off a whole decanter of wine and I slept right through 'til eight the next morning. That's when I went in. That's when I saw him." He closed his eyes. "Oh God, I can't bear this!"

He normally gets up during the night, but not that night?

Julie hugged him and silently asked herself if he was being more dramatic than usual. She held him at arm's length and looked in his eyes. "David. Do you know what the Florida papers are saying? What they've been implying?"

"Of course I do!" he said. "All the questions they asked me? But, Julie, I had nothing to do with it!" He began to cry again. "Oh, how could Marc *do* this?"

"David. Maybe he didn't do it. You said you were sleeping very soundly. Does anyone else have a key to the house?"

"No. No one," he said, blowing his nose, a picture of misery. "Just Marc and I." Julie knew how hard it was to fake sadness. She decided that David's demeanor was wholly consistent with the sensitive, emotional person she knew him to be.

"For now, we may just have to accept that he's gone and leave the rest for later," she said. "I'm concerned about *you*, though, David; about all this notoriety. I have a friend who's worked with an attorney, Jake Goldman. His office is in the Keys. He said he'd represent you if you need him. Do you know who he is?"

"I think I've heard of him," said David, unconsciously raising his hand, biting a nail. "I've been wondering if I should get a lawyer. Would it look bad, do you think?"

Julie could see that David was anxious, but she also noted that he displayed no signs of manipulation or deception.

It was a relief.

"Forget about that," she said, concerned for him. "It's a good idea for you to protect yourself, even if it's just to put someone between you and the press."

"Maybe you're right."

"Another thing, David; I was thinking that, if you don't mind, I'd like to come to Key West to stay with you for a little while. Would that be all right?"

"Oh, heavens, yes…thank you, Julie. I'm so glad you're coming!"

He looked as lost as an abandoned puppy. Julie squeezed his hand, and smiled. "I'll see you soon," she said and kissed his cheek before leaving him.

Pete and Joan were talking to some friends from Solomon Chrysler when she returned.

"Julie. It's so nice to see you after all this time. Sorry it has to be for this," said a petite, gray haired woman.

It took Julie a moment to recognize Laura Bennett. "Hello, Laura," she said. "Yes. It's horrible."

"Seems like we just see each other at funerals," said Laura. Realizing her faux pas at once, she put her hand to her mouth and said, "Oh, *my*. I'm so sorry, Julie! I didn't mean to bring up the past."

"It's okay, Laura," she said, taking her hand. "It was a long time ago."

After a little more visiting, they said their goodbyes and left for their individual cars. As Julie climbed into the Malibu and pulled in behind Pete and Joan to head back to their house, she reflected on several things she had learned at the wake. But she was bone-weary, and there was still a burial tomorrow. So, for tonight, she decided, there would be no more questions.

Everyone was in a somber mood the next morning. Even Paul and Pete, Jr. were quiet. Julie tried to talk to them a bit about school, but she mostly got one-word answers. *Ah, well*, she thought, *I'm actually a stranger to these boys.*

Julie drove Pete and Joan in the Malibu, and they joined the cortege at the funeral home. As they slowly moved out in the long line of cars, she regretted that she hadn't spoken with any of the Castle family.

"I never met any of Miriam's side of the family, the Castles. Do you know them? Did either of you speak to any of them?"

"Yeah," said Pete. "Miriam's younger brother, Matt, was there."

"Oh, yes," said Julie, who remembered Marc speaking of his "Uncle Matt".

"I talked to him," said Pete. "He was all broken up; they were close. He said Marc had called him and they'd talked just recently. Matt's partner, Tom Connor, was with him, but I didn't get a chance to talk to him. Tom's a real nice guy; never married, so no kids. He was like an uncle to Marc, too."

"Yes, that's right. He was at Marc's Newbury Street show," said Joan, nodding. "I saw Matt's wife at the wake, Julie. She was there with the older children. We said 'hi', but we didn't actually talk."

Those were the nieces and nephews Milton Solomon referred to, thought Julie.

Finally, they arrived at the gravesite and took their places around the casket. The service was more difficult to bear than Julie had expected. She tried hard not to cry, but, in the end, she couldn't help herself.

Only two other people were crying unabashedly, she noticed. One was David Harris. Julie didn't recognize the other person, an older man. The same man had appeared stricken at the wake the day before. She recalled that the Castle family had seemed to surround him. Now that she thought about it…they seemed to be comforting him.

He looks a lot like Marc.

She glanced from the man to Pete, a questioning look on her face.

Pete leaned over and whispered. "Tom Connor, Matt Castle's law partner."

23

J oan had prepared a light and easy Italian dinner, and now the three of them sat in the living room before the fireplace, finishing their wine while the boys played a video game in the den.

Julie was mulling over Joan's earlier account of her job as payroll manager at Solomon Chrysler, especially Avram's nasty, unwarranted rebuke to a perfectly sensible suggestion. Not that Pete didn't deserve it, but the timing of his promotion to GM in Lynn was bothering Julie, because it had also removed Joan from the payroll department.

"Joannie, I was wondering...while you were there, was anything else going on at the Boston dealership that struck you as odd?"

"No, not that I can think of," said Joan. "Avram was just so arrogant, you know?"

"I can think of somethin'," said Pete. "Milton Solomon was a sharp car dealer. He was a negotiator. He came up from *sales*, you know? Avram, on the other hand, doesn't know his ass from his elbow when it comes to this business. He's a friggin' bean counter, and a lousy one!"

"Pete, quiet down...the boys will hear you," said Joan.

"Okay. Sorry," said Pete, lowering his voice. "It just burns me that Avram makes all the decisions."

"What happened to Milton Solomon?" asked Julie.

"He comes in every once in a while, but Avram's in charge. The ol' man thinks Avram's a genius. What a joke! Avram does the stupidest things I've ever seen! I don't know about the other two stores, but there's barely any profit in mine because of that...jerk. Our costs for advertising, uniforms, wiper rags, floor mats, parts, paint...you name it...is sky high! And I can't do a thing about it; it's all handled by Avram in the Boston store."

"How long has that been going on?"

"For years," said Pete. "Not that *he* isn't rollin' in dough. And he likes to throw it around, too. Women, gamblin', a goddamn Jaguar! That's right. He doesn't even drive one of our cars.

"He isn't foolin' me with all his society connections and charity shit. We've expanded from one store to three, and I can't see where the money came from to do it. I wouldn't be surprised if we were washin' more than cars."

Pete leaned forward, pinching the bridge of his nose, while Joan unconsciously rubbed the back of her neck.

Julie knew at once that they'd had this conversation many times. Pete was clearly conflicted about his job, and Joan was stressed to the max, afraid he might quit.

"Well, I've got some thoughts on all of this that I want to look into," said Julie. "As much as I appreciate the hospitality, you guys, it's probably best if I leave here in the morning and spend tomorrow night in Boston. I'm planning to call Conner, Castle & Mann and make an appointment to see Marc's uncle. And, believe me, I've got some questions for Avram, too, before I leave."

Julie arose early the next morning, so she could say goodbye to the boys and Pete before they left for the day. She had expected to have breakfast with them. Wrong. It was strictly grab n' go in the Soldano household on weekdays.

"Phew!" said Joan, as Pete, the last to leave, went out through the garage door, mobile-coffee-cup in hand. "What a zoo, huh?"

"They could use you at Starbucks," said Julie, waving goodbye to Pete as she entered the kitchen from the garage.

She had just come in from walking Paul and Pete, Jr. out front to the street. She had carried her coffee with her. Warming her hands on the mug, she had leaned against the Malibu and watched the boys as they walked down the steep little hill to their bus stop at the bottom. Julie could see the river through the trees, sparkling in the sun. When the school bus picked up the boys, she'd gone back in the house.

Now the two women settled down in peace at the kitchen table.

"It's so good to see you, Julie. I've thought of you so much over the years."

"I should have called," said Julie, looking down at the table. "I'm sorry, Joannie. There's really no excuse. In the beginning, after Dan died..."

"Julie, it's all right," said Joan, interrupting. "I understand. You don't have to explain anything."

"No. I want to," said Julie. "It's time I did." She took a breath and continued.

"After Dan died, I couldn't bear to see anybody or talk about it. I couldn't face his family, our friends. If Marc hadn't been so dogged...so persistent...I probably would have cut him off, too. Over time...well...it was just easier to keep it that way.

"The truth is...I'm responsible for Dan's death."

"But that's absurd, Julie! From what I know, you nearly drowned yourself trying to save him!"

"No. Dan drowned because I didn't get to him fast enough." To Julie's chagrin, a tear spilled over and ran down her cheek.

Joan reached across the table with some napkins, and took her hand. "Honey, here... listen to me. It wasn't your fault."

"It was…it was," said Julie, sniffing.

"Sh-h, now," said Joan. "Something you should know, Julie. I've been to that island."

Julie looked at her, surprised.

"That's right. It was after you moved to Florida. Milt and Miriam offered it to Pete and me for our honeymoon. The fact is we were broke, so we took it gladly.

"Anyhow, what you need to know is that we rode over to the eastern shore. We stood on that very point! And I'm telling you, hon, we could see that rip current clearly. Pete threw a branch in, and it took it out in a flash! It's a wonder you didn't die, too, jumping in there after him like that."

"I dove in right away, but I didn't swim, Joan. That's what I did wrong: *I didn't swim.* The current was so fast; it seemed faster than I could swim. I thought it would take me to him, but it was moving Dan at the same speed! I should have been swimming as strong as I could, like walking fast on the moving walkway at the airport. *I did the wrong thing.*"

"Julie…honey…how could you possibly have known what to do? It was a freak situation, a split second decision. Besides, have you ever considered the possibility that Dan drowned before you ever dove into the water?"

It was a simple thought:

Dan was dead the whole time.

Julie had suppressed that horrible, simple thought during her rescue attempt. Afterward, she had blocked it to make sense of her foolhardy action. It was crystal clear now that she had run away from anyone who might make her face the truth about it. But time had done its job. In fact, Julie felt as if a great weight had been lifted from her shoulders.

"Julie?"

"Yes," she said. "You're right, Joan. Dan *was* probably dead when he washed out of that cave. I just couldn't face that years ago. You're a good friend. Thank you for being so direct."

Okay, enough, thought Julie, emotionally spent. *I can't talk about this anymore.* With a final sigh, she squeezed Joan's hand and changed the subject. "I apologize for my absence all these years, Joannie. I promise to be a much better friend in the future. Speaking of the future, have you guys decided where the boys are going to school? Are you thinking U-Mass, Boston College, or what?"

Her awkward segue worked.

The two of them went on to talk about the boys and the University of Massachusetts, about local politics and tennis. Their conversation was easy and enjoyable. The years melted away.

All too soon, it was time for Julie to leave. She wanted to get checked into the Marriott Long Wharf in Boston before noon. Her plan was to see Matt Castle shortly after that and she didn't want to miss him.

Joan walked her to her car and they hugged.

Julie turned the ignition, waved to her friend, and released the emergency brake.

The Malibu started forward…too fast. Julie put her foot on the brake and it went all the way to the floor. She stamped on it, futilely.

What the hell?!

The car hurtled down the steep hill, headed straight for the river.

24

Instinctively, Julie slammed on the emergency brake and pushed the automatic gearshift to *Park*. She yanked the steering wheel hard to the left and held it there. In a matter of seconds, the car had reached the two lane road and done a one-eighty to the left before slamming to a stop, rear-end facing the river.

In shock and trying to catch her breath, Julie closed her eyes and dropped her head on her arms, slumped over the steering wheel. Mere moments later, she lifted her head and looked out her window.

There was a car heading right for her.

Shit, shit, SHIT!

She saw the driver's panicked face and heard the squeal of his brakes. She closed her eyes tight, bracing and holding her breath, expecting the broadside impact...

It didn't happen! The man had stopped the car a few inches from her door! The older driver was looking at her, agape, relief written all over his face. Julie exhaled like the governor just called off her execution.

Thank you, God! Thank you!

She heard another screech as a second hapless motorist just missed hitting the old man. Unable to open the driver's side door, she slid to the right and jumped out of the Malibu.

Joan Soldano had watched the accident in horror, running down the hill after the runaway car. Now, she darted across the road. "Ohmigod, ohmigod! Julie! Are you all right?!"

"I'm okay! The brakes are gone!"

The white-haired, bespectacled old man that had almost T-boned Julie had gotten out of his car. "Are you okay, Miss?"

"Yes, thank God. Are you?"

"Yes, I'm just glad I was able to stop!"

The back end of Julie's car had knocked down a section of the low stone wall edging the river bank and smacked into a tree directly behind it. The rear end was caved in and two tires were blown.

Julie saw a police car, weaving through the traffic, heading in her direction. She realized then that she had to get the Malibu off the narrow road as quickly as possible. The car was only partially blocking the northbound lane and people were slowing down and going around it. But behind the older man's car, the traffic was stacking up. She dug out her cell phone and her rental contract and called Hertz.

Once the report was made and the car towed away, Julie followed Joan back up Drake Hill to the house. The plan was for Joan to drive her to the local Hertz office for a replacement. Pausing by the front walk to rest from tugging her carry-on up the hill, she happened to glance down at the small bag. The wheels had left two short, dark stripes on the pavement leading to a tiny iridescent pool.

A puddle of brake fluid.

25

Given that she was still alive and breathing, Julie decided not to press her luck by asking God for a parking space. She left the new rental - a Camry - at the Marriott, and walked up State Street for her one-thirty appointment with Matt Castle.

Entering the lobby of the building, Julie noticed that the law firm was the only occupant of the top floor. She took the elevator up and stepped out into a large reception area. It was designed to impress: large oriental carpets atop highly polished hardwood floors and Old English mahogany furniture. There was a gold sign on the wall facing the elevator:

CONNOR, CASTLE & MANN

A dignified older woman sat at a desk to the right. She smiled as Julie approached. "Good afternoon. May I help you?"

"Yes. I'm Julie O'Hara. I'm here to see Mr. Castle. I have an appointment."

The woman glanced at her computer.

"Oh, yes, Ms. O'Hara," she said. "Mr. Castle is expecting you. Would you have a seat? I'll let him know that you're here. Please help yourself to the coffee over there."

Julie passed on the coffee; she was jittery enough from her 'accident' in Salem.

Matt Castle came out to meet her almost immediately, and she remembered him from the funeral. He was a tall man in a dark gray pinstriped suit with an impeccable shirt and tie. His hair was turning gray at the temples which gave him a solid, patrician air. He welcomed her warmly.

"Ms. O'Hara?" he said, extending his hand. "I'm Matthew Castle. Please call me Matt. It's a pleasure to finally meet Marc's best friend, Merlin. He never ceased bragging about you."

"Please, call me Julie," she said, shaking his hand. "Marc was becoming so well known that I was the one bragging about being his friend. I know he cared a great deal for you, too, Matt. He spoke of you many times. I'm so sorry for your loss."

"Thank you," he said. "Come, let's go to my office."

Julie followed him down a hallway past smaller offices to a large, windowed corner suite. The overall impression was English Hunt Club: crimson leather on polished dark wood, oil landscapes and hunting prints.

The walls were filled with law books and accreditation, family photos artfully interspersed.

Rather than sitting opposite her at his desk, he led her to a pair of club chairs.

"Julie. I'm going to be frank with you," he said, unbuttoning his suit jacket and taking a seat. "I'm deeply suspicious about my nephew's death. Marc was not at all suicidal."

Julie's impression of Matt Castle as an ally was all but confirmed with those words.

"No, he wasn't," said Julie. "Marc and I discussed the subject once. He was emphatic about suicide being cowardly. He specifically said that it was cruel to loved ones who were left behind. He would never have taken his own life."

"Do you think it could have been an accident?" asked Matt. "Did you know it was an injection?"

"I just learned that," said Julie, "but I don't know what it was."

"They told me it was oxycodone."

"Oxycodone? There's no way this was an accident! I think Marc was murdered."

"Yes," said Matt, "so do I."

They were quiet for a moment, the enormity of that sinking in.

"There's something else, Matt. Someone tried to kill me this morning."

His eyes widened in shock and concern.

Julie recounted her close call, in all its harrowing detail.

"Someone tampered with your brakes?"

"Yes. I'm certain of it. It was a new car; the brake pedal was high, tight. I drove the car for three days and the brakes worked fine."

"Did you report it to the police?"

"Just an accident report, when the police showed up on the road. I didn't see the brake fluid in front of Pete's house until later."

"Who do you think…?"

Aghast, his unfinished question hung in the air.

"It had to be someone who knew I was suspicious. Someone who knew exactly where I was staying, who knew where the Soldanos live in Salem. Someone who knew they had to act fast, because I wouldn't be there long." Julie paused, looking at Matt. "Let's just say that Avram Solomon is at the top of my short list."

"Why Avram?"

"Because I saw through his act and I think he knows it. I know he lies all the time, because he's smooth. It takes practice to be a good liar. But there are always leaks: tiny facial movements, a gesture, the pitch of one's voice, their pattern of speech. No one can control them all. Avram certainly wasn't grieving, Matt. What's more, I believe he's hiding something."

"Well, he's capable of anything, in my opinion," said Matt. "But as for Marc's death…I know for a fact that Avram was here in Boston when it happened. It was the first thing I verified, Julie."

She nodded.

"I know Marc hated him."

She remembered her earlier conversation with Joan. "I was wondering about Castle Cay, Matt. Who owns the island?"

"Marc did. He inherited it from my sister, Miriam. He never used it. Since my sister died there in 1993, none of us have."

He tilted his head in sympathy.

"I was sorry to hear about your husband, Julie."

"Thank you. I was sorry about Miriam, too. I think that place is cursed."

He nodded, and continued.

"Marc did, too. In fact, he wanted to sell it. He called me a few weeks ago and said he'd had a good offer from Holiday Cruise Lines for it. "

"What? He was seeking your advice about a sale? Of Castle Cay?"

"Yes. It was a large amount of money."

"Can you tell me any more about it?" asked Julie. "It would help me if I knew what questions he had and what you advised him."

Matt thought about it for a moment.

"I don't see why not," he said.

"Holiday offered $40 million for Castle Cay. Avram had called Marc to tell him. And, as you know, Marc never trusted Avram about anything. So, he called me. He said that Avram seemed very eager for him to sell, and he wondered why. I said that perhaps Avram was sick of managing the property, or he might have felt the money would be better invested elsewhere."

"Do you know who the listing agent was?"

"Yes, I do. Wait a minute…"

He got up, went to his desk, and pulled out a piece of paper that was tucked under the clear mat.

"It was listed with Island World Realty. They're in Miami. Marc said they specialized in islands and waterfront properties."

"How did he find them?"

"I don't think he did. I think Avram probably listed it."

"But you said that Marc wanted to sell?"

"Yes. But, keep in mind, Marc hadn't been there for years. He was thinking that perhaps he should go there again before deciding. On the other hand, he didn't want to delay and lose the buyer. So that was the quandary."

"What did you advise him?"

"It was a low offer. I told him not to rush into it! I said that if he felt he should go there first, then that's what he should do. I don't know if he went or not, though."

"Have you talked to Avram Solomon about any of this?"

"No, I haven't," he said. "But I received a letter from him about Marc's trust fund. It was to inform me that Avram, as trustee, was completing an inventory and that the trust would be 'liquidated as soon as possible'.

He said that when it was ready to close, he would 'make distributions to all the beneficiaries'."

"Who is the primary beneficiary?"

"I am," he said, simply.

Surprised, Julie instantly assessed his body language. He had shrugged slightly and opened his hands toward her. There was no inconsistency in any of it. Matt Castle was an honest man, and one who was already quite wealthy.

"Any idea why Avram wanted the island sold?" she asked.

"No. But I'm a lot more suspicious about it now than I was."

"There's one last thing I want to ask you, Matt. It's personal. I'll understand if you'd rather not answer. Is it possible that Milton Solomon was not Marc's father?"

Matt shifted and sighed. He leaned back in his chair. "There's no point in keeping that secret any longer, I guess. My partner, Tom Connor, is…*was...* Marc's father. God knows he wanted to tell him! But he promised my sister years ago that he wouldn't. The hell of it is, we had talked recently and he was planning to tell him. Now he'll never have the chance.

"It was all because of my sister's delusion about her sons bonding. Of course, Miriam never recognized Avram's duplicity. She didn't want to see it. No, it was her goal for them to be close. She thought it would only separate them more to know they had different fathers."

"Joan Soldano mentioned that Miriam left everything to Marc?"

"Oh, no," said Matt. "Miriam left an equal amount of money to her sons. The island was an additional bequest in Marc's trust. And that was fair. At the time, you see, Milton was clearly putting Solomon Chrysler into Avram's hands.

"Miriam saw Marc as being on 'her side' of the family. I don't think she thought about the monetary value of Castle Cay at all. I don't think she ever imagined the island being sold; her intent was simply to keep it in the Castle family.

"As for Marc's trust fund, Miriam's reasoning was that Avram was an accountant and he cared about the family money... where Marc clearly didn't. In her mind, she was protecting Marc by appointing Avram trustee.

"It was a terrible idea. I tried to talk her out of it, but she wouldn't listen to a word I said. In the end, she and Milton went to another firm to draw up their estate plans. Of course, after Miriam died, we lost all of their business...but that was years ago."

"Why was that?"

"Avram chose Cardenas and Shaw."

"Where have I seen that name?"

"In the newspapers, perhaps. No doubt you've heard of their clients? The Tambini family here in Boston?"

Shit, thought Julie.

Up to my ankles.

Julie called the airport as she hurried back to the Marriott, reserving a seat on the eight o'clock flight to Miami. She also made a reservation there at the Holiday Inn. Then she went to her room, threw everything into her carry-on and headed for the door.

Wait...

She picked up the hotel phone and recorded some misdirection:

"Sorry I missed you! I'll be back later."

One more stop and I'm out of here!

26

The traffic in Boston was chaotic, the city a maze of one-way streets. When at last Julie neared Solomon Chrysler's original store, the area began to look familiar, if more cramped. The dealership, in particular, seemed much smaller than when she had worked there...a common trick of memory. She pulled into the crowded car lot, recalling Joan's words, *"The Lynn and Waltham stores are much larger"*.

Julie didn't recognize any of the salesmen jockeying for position. One of them, a slick-looking young man, came out to greet her.

"Hi! Welcome to Solomon Chrysler. How can I help you today?"

"Sorry, but you can't. I'm not looking for a car. I'm here to see Avram Solomon. Is he in?"

"Yes, he is. Go on in."

"Is he still in the front office?" she asked, figuring Avram must have moved into Milton's private office with the big one-way mirrored wall that looked out on the sales action.

"Yep, right over there," he said, opening the door and pointing.

Julie thanked him and quickly crossed the showroom floor, hoping Avram hadn't seen her. She turned down the hallway and knocked on the first door on the right.

"Yes, what is it?" said Avram.

"A visitor," said Julie, opening the door and sticking her head in, all smiles.

His shock was obvious.

"Julie…good to see you!" he said, quickly regaining his composure.

Avram looked like a stock broker, not a car dealer. His dark hair was combed smoothly back. He wore leather suspenders over a crisp white shirt, and his silk tie sported an elegant Windsor knot.

Julie had interrupted him while he was discussing something with one of the service managers. He dismissed the man. "Go ahead and do the job for them, Richard. Got to keep the customers happy," he said, ushering him out.

The man left, shaking his head.

Julie noticed that Avram's office was designed to reflect the stature of its occupant. It looked like the chamber of a pompous judge. His desk was grand, with an equally imposing chair behind it, larger and higher than the two in front of the desk. There were pictures of him with dignitaries, but no family pictures were in sight.

"So, Julie," he said, assuming his throne and directing her to a chair opposite him, "this is an unexpected pleasure."

Julie noted his posture. He sought to give her an impression of relaxation. He leaned back in his chair and smiled but, at the same time, he made a high steeple with his hands. Just the fingertips were touching. It was a smug gesture, creating a wall between them. Further, there was controlled aggression in his eyes.

"Yes, I wanted to spend an extra night in town," she said. "So many memories here in Boston, especially at Solomon Chrysler. I just thought I'd drop in and say hello, for old times' sake."

"Well, that's wonderful! Perhaps we could have dinner," he said, smiling and leaning forward. "Where are you staying?"

From an expert's point of view, Julie appreciated Avram's smooth transition. *He actually looks and sounds genuine now. He's fascinating,* she thought. And reminded herself… *like a cobra.*

"I'm at the Marriott Long Wharf, but I'm planning to do a little shopping and turn in early," she said apologetically.

"You and I didn't get much time to talk about Marc at the wake, Avram. I was so stunned by his death. He was a very good friend of mine, as you know. Of course, I'm not a family member, but I thought…if I could find out just a *few* more details…it would give me closure, you know?"

"Of course," said Avram, visibly relieved.

The steeple is lower. Good. We're playing nice now.

"How can I help?" he said.

"I was wondering, Avram; you went down to see Marc just before I did. Did he seem depressed to you?" asked Julie, assuming the visit.

"Yes, he did, I'm sorry to say."

"Even though his career was going so well and he'd just been offered $40 million for Castle Cay?"

Avram's dark eyes were riveted, burning through her. He picked up a Mont Blanc pen from the desk and began turning it, end over end, in his right hand. Sardonically, the bottom half of his face kept smiling.

"Yes," he said. "Even so."

I can't believe it; he's displaying superiority. Like this is some kind of game. We'll see about that.

"It's quite a coincidence, after so many years of owning Castle Cay, that Marc gets a multi-million dollar offer to buy the island and suddenly ends up dead, don't you think?"

That did it.

"Listen to me, *Merlin*," he said, standing, signaling that their meeting was over. He jabbed the Mont Blanc at her like a bayonet with each point he was making. "Not that it's any of your *business*, but that sale is done.

And further, Marc's estate goes to my *uncle*, Matthew Castle, and *not* to me. I am merely the trustee. So, unless you have a *legitimate* question regarding my brother's suicide, I think I've helped you all I can with your...*closure*."

"I'm sorry, Avram," said Julie, rising and feigning apology. "I didn't mean to imply anything. I just found the timing curious. I know, of course, that you were here in Boston when Marc died; I'm sure it was a terrible shock. By the way, do you happen to know Roland Archer or Susan Dwyer?"

"Yes, it *was* a shock," said Avram, holding the door open, glaring at her. "And certainly, I know Marc's agent. I don't know the other person. Now, if you don't mind, I really am busy."

Julie said goodbye and walked out to the Camry.

You were shocked, all right, Avram.

When you saw ME.

27

"What the hell did you expect me to do? Run her off the road like they do in the movies? Make her car go up in flames on Route One? I'm a mechanic, not a fucking stunt man! You wanted 'an accident'. That's what you got."

"What I got was nothing!"

Avram slammed the phone down. He fell back into his chair. A furious scowl twisted his face as he obsessively turned the pen in his hand.

Why can't she mind her own business?

He took a deep breath, and exhaled.

She doesn't matter. She's not going to affect the deal with Holiday.

Avram slipped on his tailored jacket, carefully tucking the pen into the inside pocket. He stepped out of his office, locking the door behind him.

"I'm leaving now, Barbara. I'll be in tomorrow."

"Yes, Mr. Solomon," said the office manager.

He ignored the sales activity as he crossed the showroom floor. He was headed for his Jaguar, blatantly parked front and center outside, much to the consternation of his own salesmen.

Sliding in behind the wheel for the short drive to his Beacon Hill townhouse, thoughts of Julie O'Hara intermingled with Avram's plans for the evening. He had a call girl coming to his house and he was looking forward to it. She wasn't going to enjoy it, but that was the point, wasn't it? Otherwise, he wouldn't have to pay her. *Too bad it wasn't O'Hara.*

Avram was a dangerous man. And he was fully aware of it. The epiphany had taken place when he was eleven. It began with a fight. He chuckled, remembering it.

I beat up the fag. I caught him in my bedroom.

Marc, who was eight, had to be taken to the hospital. They had recommended that Avram get some help with "anger management".

After several visits and tests, the psychiatrist had telephoned his mother. Avram had picked up the bedroom extension as soon as he'd heard his mother say, "*Oh, hello, Dr. Weissman…*"

The doctor proceeded to tell her that, in his opinion, Avram was a sociopath and not likely to change. The doctor apologized about having to give her such an "unwelcome diagnosis". He suggested that she might want to get a second opinion. Oddly - to Avram - his mother never took him to another shrink and never mentioned Dr. Weissman's call to his father.

The very next day, he had looked up the word *sociopath* in the school library. It was enlightening. Simply put, Avram didn't care about other people. He could hurt them without "caring" about it, and they sensed it. It was just a confirmation, really. Avram had always noticed the fear in their eyes, how they moved out of his way. But now he knew why. He was wired differently, and he was glad. But he was also smart. This was an advantage that had to be handled carefully. Although he enjoyed thinking of himself as a lone wolf, he saw the advantage of *pretending* to be like the sheep and deliberately set about deceiving his parents, particularly his mother. He controlled himself with Marc thereafter, too.

He smiled, disdain etched on his face.

The psychiatric literature said that people like him had no "moral compass".

He laughed out loud.

They didn't realize that he was North on their stupid compass and they were all simply relative to that.

Or not.

Life had evolved into a sophisticated game for Avram. Moving among the sheep and manipulating them.

Of course, the money was important. The player with the biggest pile was the winner. And so far, Avram had over $6 million in the Caymans.

He chuckled.

I win.

28

After a fitful night at the airport hotel in Miami, Julie sat on the edge of the bed in her underwear. She had called Luz, who had told her everything was cool with Sol. Julie had explained that she needed to go to the Keys, and that she'd be staying with David. However, as a precaution, she had instructed Luz to tell anyone that called that she was in Chicago at a conference.

She had also asked her to look up something.

Luz called back a couple minutes later. She had pulled up the *Island World Realty* listing Julie had requested. The agent's name was Frank Martino. Julie had already called and made a morning appointment with the man, saying simply that she "wanted to talk about an island".

Now she sat there, literally on edge, her cell phone in her left hand, her chin in her right and her bare feet drumming away on the carpet.

I need him. I really do.

She took a calming breath and keyed in the number. It rang.

Once.

Twice.

"Hello?"

"Joe? It's Julie. I need your help."

29

Three years ago, Joe Garrett didn't know he was in love with Julie O'Hara.

And then she walked through his office door.

Joe had *seen* Julie bite her lower lip that certain way, *seen* that elusive smile before. Her hair was tied back, but he knew at once what it looked like loose. And there was more…

He had tried to analyze it. Did Julie O'Hara just happen to fit some unconscious image he'd constructed? In the end, it didn't matter.

Joe was bowled over by the déjà vu.

After a reasonable period, he had tried to let Julie know how he felt. But every attempt backfired. He flirted…and she ran for the shrubs like a feral cat. While it was true that Joe wasn't used to being rebuffed, the deal with Julie was particularly confusing.

There was something between them, and he was sure she felt it, too. The more this odd push/pull magnetism continued, the more caught he was, like a moon circling a planet...unable to get closer but unable to get free.

Joe thought about their odd relationship once again, as he gulped down his morning coffee and set the empty mug on the kitchen bar. The door beside it was open to allow the morning air to come in through the screen.

He had been remodeling the second floor by himself, a little at a time, the operative word being *little.* So far, he'd opened up two interior walls and re-laid the oak flooring, but there was still that unfinished, unfurnished look about the place and a smell of raw wood and paint.

The kitchen Joe stood in had been installed first, so that he could live up there while he completed the two first-floor offices. The irony struck him.

So Merlin and I could have separate spaces.

Joe could hardly believe that she had finally called him.

Now, worried and occupied with her case, he couldn't move fast enough. He closed and locked the back door and strode down the hall.

Joe stepped into the shower, shivering as the cold spray hit his body. Facing the round mirror stuck on the tile, he quickly brushed his teeth. He ran his hand over the stubble on his chin and decided to pass on shaving, since he'd probably be out of there before the water even warmed up.

Soon, he was out of the apartment and headed downstairs. He needed to talk to his secretary and make a couple calls before he left for the airport.

He found her in the office, standing on a chair, reaching for a chain attached to the ceiling fan. Janet Hawkins was a wise-cracking, petite and busty blonde on the sunny side of fifty. She was wearing slacks, for which Joe was very grateful, considering her position. "Hi, honey, I'm home," he said…his usual greeting.

"Good. Hang on to this chair before I kill myself. Really, Joe, a woman my age needs this thing on High! Why do you keep turning it down?"

"Because, dear, it blows my papers all around."

"You're hardly ever here, and I'm *always* here. How about if you just shut it off on the wall switch when you're working in the office?"

"I can do that. Here, let me help you down."

"Thanks. So what's up?"

"I'm not going to be around for the next few days," said Joe, sitting down at the big oak desk that once belonged to his father. He grabbed his card file. "You know that friend of Merlin's who died in Key West? Marc Solomon, the artist?"

"Yeah?" said Janet, peering at him over her glasses.

"She called me. She thinks he was murdered. I'm going to help her. I'm going to Miami and then I'm meeting her in Key West, but I'll keep in touch."

Joe knew from Janet's expression of wide-eyed innocence that she couldn't wait to discuss this development with Julie's assistant, Luz.

"What?"

"Nothing," said Joe. "Have we heard from Johnson & Cummings?"

"Yup. The check came in yesterday," she said. "I deposited it. $8,600.00."

"Hallelujah!"

Joe had been waiting for that case to settle.

"What else?"

"Angela called a couple of times," said Janet, offering the information like a glass of sour milk.

Angela D'Amato was Joe's ex-girlfriend. He broke up with Angie two years ago when he became hopelessly attracted to his new tenant. He told her he thought they should "see other people". Of course, the only person Joe wanted to see was Julie.

But that didn't happen. Joe really tried to avoid Angie…but sometimes he didn't try too hard. Janet didn't approve.

"I'll call her later," he said, flipping through the card file.

He found the one he was looking for:

Sawyer Aerial Photography

Will Sawyer was a pilot that Joe had met when he was in the service. He was a few years older than Joe, but they were both Florida boys away from home, and they had become good friends.

Joe punched in the number.

Will's wife, Carolyn, answered the phone. Joe talked to her politely for a minute or so, before asking for Will.

"Hey, Buddy!" said Will, "How's it going?"

"I'm good," said Joe. "How's everything down in Miami?"

"Great! When are you coming down? We'll pull up some bugs!"

Will had a boat; Joe went down every so often to help him with lobster traps.

Joe told him about Julie's case, particularly about the growing significance of the island, Castle Cay.

"So, I was hoping I could hire you to take me there, get some photos?"

"When?" asked Will.

"As soon as you can."

Will paused. Joe waited.

"Tomorrow's Saturday and I'm open," he said at last. "There's a tropical depression southeast of Haiti. That's far enough away, but you never know in hurricane season. It may ground me pretty soon. How fast can you get here?"

"I can be there this afternoon," said Joe.

"Yeah, okay. And Joe, I'll only charge you for my costs."

Joe closed his eyes and pumped his fist.

All right!

"Thanks, Will. I'll grab a cab to your house from the airport. See you later."

Joe hung up and reached for his card file again to look up Sherman Dixon's number. He located the card and rang the number.

Long time since I talked to Sherman...

Sherman and Joe had gone to Florida State University together. What a time that was! They were campus heroes. It was all about babes, booze and football. Their senior year of college was a continuous party. Sherman graduated and went into the FBI.

Joe graduated and went into rehab.

Joe remembered his mother going nuts over his decision to join the navy after getting out of there. He would never forget his father's sharp rebuke: "Let him go, Dot! It'll make a man out of him." How he had hated Big Joe for saying that. Of course, his father had been right on the money.

"Dixon, here."

"Hi, Sherm. It's Joe Garrett."

"Joe! Good to hear from you! Did you see the game last Saturday?"

Joe knew he was talking about FSU. Sherm was still a huge Seminole fan, even though he didn't live in Florida anymore.

Joe could picture the big black man standing in front of the TV in the den, yelling, "GO! GO!" at the FSU quarterback while his wife and two little girls looked on, mystified.

Joe said he'd missed the game, and filled Sherman in on Julie's case.

"I'm thinking about this guy, Avram Solomon, the dead man's brother," Joe said. "Just thinking…but maybe the brother is involved with the Tambini family up there, and maybe it somehow connects to the death in Key West.

"I mean, Julie was really close to this guy, Sherm, and she's a hundred percent sure he didn't kill himself. Now, I know you can't tell me anything about any ongoing cases, and I wouldn't ask you to," said Joe. "But I thought you might be able to just check out the name for me, see if it's come up before. Is that possible?"

"Sure, I guess I can do that. You want me to call you after I check him out?"

"That'd be great."

He gave Sherm his cell number, spelled out Avram's name, and gave him the address of the Boston dealership. They talked a bit more, promising to get together soon, and hung up.

Last, Joe called the airlines for the next flight to Miami and booked a seat.

"Okay," he said to Janet, rising. "I'm off. I'll see you when I see you."

Joe ran up the stairs, two at a time. He quickly went around the apartment, gathering up his stuff. Finally, his carry-on at his feet, he sat down on the couch to make one more call.

"Angie? Look, before you say anything… there's something I've got to tell you…"

30

J ulie sat in the back seat of the taxi thinking about David Harris. It was Friday, September 21st, and she planned to be on the one o'clock flight out of Miami to Key West. David was all set to pick her up there.

She thought about what Joe had told her: "*There was no forced entry*". She reminded herself that David was the only other person in the house when Marc died. But it was no use; no matter how she looked at it, she couldn't imagine David having anything to do with Marc's death.

She got out of the cab a few storefronts down from Island World Realty, which, fortunately, was fairly close to Miami International. Julie tipped the driver a twenty. He was to come back for her in precisely one hour, if he wanted to collect another one.

She was surprised to find the place in a strip mall. There were a few guys in cubicles on phones and computers, and an older woman was sitting at a desk up front, near the door. It suddenly occurred to Julie that they probably didn't have much *walk-in* business for multimillion-dollar islands. Obviously, the closings took place somewhere else.

"Can I help you?"

"Yes. I'm looking for Frank Martino."

A dark haired guy, late twenties maybe, rolled his desk chair backwards into the aisle between the cubes. He looked at Julie, a pleased smile on his face.

"Hi! You Julie O'Hara?"

"Yes. Frank Martino?"

"That's me. I'll be right with you."

Slick. The Bluetooth phone in his ear completes the image…

Julie was glad she hadn't mentioned Castle Cay specifically. She had merely said that she was "flying into Miami from Boston," and "wanted to talk about an island." She wanted to gauge his reaction in person.

"You want to get some lunch? There's a sub shop next door," said Martino.

"I could use a cup of coffee," said Julie, and followed him out. As they walked to the nearby sub shop, Julie noticed some expensive cars parked in front of Island World…a BMW convertible, a Cadillac and a Lexus.

They got their orders, and sat down opposite each other in a booth.

"So how's the real estate business these days?" asked Julie.

"In the tank, I hear," said Martino, smiling. "But not islands. They don't lose value like regular property and the buyers are always qualified. So, are you a buyer or a seller?"

"Neither, I'm afraid," said Julie, watching him carefully. "I'm here to talk about Castle Cay in the Abacos...and Marc Solomon."

Martino's body stiffened immediately. He was surprised and definitely unhappy. He was frowning, his brows knit together.

The deal with Holiday Cruise Lines hasn't closed yet, I bet...and he has a big stake in it.

I wonder how much?

"Who are you? What does that have to do with you?" Martino asked, no longer interested in his sandwich.

"I don't have anything to do with it. Marc Solomon was my friend, that's all. That's why I'm here. This sale just happens to coincide with his death. I only want to ask a few questions, Frank, just public record things," Julie said, sipping her coffee.

"What kind of questions?"

"Well, I already know quite a bit about it. I know it was listed for $45 million, and that Holiday Cruise Lines has offered $40 million."

"Yeah. So?" said Martino.

I knew it. The deal isn't done.

"And you are both the listing and selling agent, right?" said Julie.

"So what?" said Martino.

So that gives you a lot of motive to see this deal done...one way or another.

"Oh, nothing, really," said Julie, smiling. "Good for you! I know how tough the real estate business can be. So how did Avram Solomon come to list it with you, anyway?"

"Um, I don't know. Somebody referred him, I guess," said Martino.

He's looking away from me. Besides, any real estate agent would remember who referred a client with a property like this.

"How long was it on the market?"

"About a year, I guess," said Martino, getting agitated. "Look, if you're really an agent, Ms. O'Hara, you can forget it. This is an exclusive listing and Castle Cay is under contract."

"I'm not a real estate agent, but aren't you forgetting something? The man who signed your deal is dead."

"That doesn't change a thing. I mean, I'm sorry about your friend, but Avram Solomon has authority to sell Castle Cay on behalf of the trust."

No doubt. But why is it so important to him? What does Avram have to gain?

It seemed that every time Julie learned something, she came away with more questions. The timing of the sale of Castle Cay was disturbing, certainly not a coincidence. She concealed her frustration and smiled at the agent.

"Well, Frank, I guess that covers it. I wish you luck with the sale, I hope it all goes well. It doesn't appear to have any connection to Marc Solomon's death."

Martino relaxed a little. He wrapped up his sandwich and stood.

"Well, I've got to get back to work. Sorry about your friend," he said.

"Thank you, and thanks for your help," said Julie.

"Yeah, sure," said Martino as he headed out the door.

Julie walked slowly to the end of the strip mall. The cabbie was punctual, and dropped her off in plenty of time to get a sandwich before boarding the small commuter plane. She hadn't realized how hungry she was.

Before long, she was in the air, headed for Key West.

31

"What did you tell her?" demanded Avram, as he held the cell phone to his ear, pacing furiously back and forth in the living room of his townhouse in Boston.

"Nothing," said Frank Martino. "She already knew the basic facts."

"Like what?" he snarled.

"Public record stuff, like the listing price and the amount Holiday offered. I think she was wondering how your brother's death affected the sale," said Frank, quickly adding, "but don't worry! I told her that you had full authority to accept the offer. Oh, I told her it was an exclusive listing, too," said Frank.

You didn't need to tell her anything, you fool, thought Avram.

"What else?"

"That's all. Oh, yeah, she wanted to know how you got my name, but I told her I didn't know. Really, that was it! She was only here five minutes and she was gone. I just thought you should know."

"All right. Thank you for calling to tell me. Listen, why is this deal taking so long, Frank?" asked Avram.

"Holiday Cruise Line is a big outfit," said Frank. "Their attorneys want to make sure that everything is in order. There won't be any problem, I assure you. We should have a closing date in Miami sometime next week."

"All right, then. Let me know as soon as you know when," said Avram. "Goodbye."

"Of course," said Frank, "goodbye."

Avram snapped the phone shut.

Well at least he wasn't stupid enough to mention Guy Tambini.

I could have given this to anyone! I don't need this connection! I should have hung up on this asshole when he called me looking for the listing.

Right.

Tell Guy Tambini's nephew to go screw himself. That would have gone over big! thought Avram. *It's a pain in the ass dealing with these hoodlums.*

Profitable, though…

A slight smile left Avram's face as rapidly as it appeared.

I hope Guy doesn't give me any shit when it's time to get out. A couple more years, that's all I need. Ten million. A nice round number. I don't know; I may not be able to use the stores that long.

I need this mess over Marc to go away. It's fucking Murphy's Law.

His cell phone rang.

"Hello?"

Avram smiled, the mask automatically taking over his features.

"Oh, hi!" he said, cheerfully.

As he listened to the caller, the smile froze into a hard line.

"You know how important this is to me," he said. "I know you don't understand…but you *promised* me!"

32

David was waiting for her at the Key West Airport. They hugged, happy to see one another, and loaded Julie's bag into the trunk of David's lime-green Volkswagen convertible. Julie refrained, once again, from asking about the big, yellow sunflower attached to the dashboard in a bud vase. Did it come with the car? Or was it his personal bit of élan?

"Oh, God! I'm *so* glad you're here at last, Julie. *No one* wants to come to the house because of all the reporters. You know we *always* had company. I'm not used to being alone like this! I miss Marc *so-o* terribly. And people *stared* at me in the Fresh Market this morning," he said, tears brimming.

Poor David. At some point in your life, you stepped out of the closet and directly onto the stage.

David's over-the-top despair was actually reassuring. Julie knew it was part of his persona. He was distraught and sad…and that was hard to fake.

"It won't last forever, David," she said, squeezing his hand. "Why were you shopping? Are you cooking tonight, I hope?"

"Veal chops and polenta with leeks", he sniffled, "with strawberry shortcake for dessert." More sniffles.

"I love strawberry shortcake!" she said.

Julie continued to steer the conversation to more soothing subjects, the warm weather, new and interesting restaurants that had opened. She asked David about some recent decorating he and Marc had done. Before long, his mood had lifted, the short ride was over, and they were pulling into the driveway behind Marc's old Volkswagen van. David was relieved to see that there were no reporters in sight.

"Thank you, God!" he said.

A few royal palms and a couple of short, bushy sego palms graced the front yard and swished in the warm breeze as they retrieved Julie's bag from the trunk of the car.

Twelve Gulf Wind Drive was a sturdy looking, white brick ranch with a circular drive and a neat lawn. Nobody expected what they saw when they stepped into the unassuming house. The view across the open floor plan was a stunning surprise. Floor to ceiling windows and two sets of clear French doors opened out onto a beautifully landscaped pool and patio. Beyond that, there was a wide canal…and usually one or two spectacular mega-yachts.

Marc and David had pooled their money and bought the house roughly ten years ago for a half million, if

Julie's memory served. *Joe said it's worth over two million now,* she recalled.

The house sat one lot away from the Gulf of Mexico, and that lot was the side yard of an estate worth *fourteen* million. Essentially, nothing between Marc and David's house and the Gulf but an expanse of green lawn, dotted with palm trees and their neighbor's sprawling free-form pool.

It was originally an ordinary three bedroom with the master at the left rear of the house opening onto the pool, and the other two bedrooms on the right end of the house, the living areas in between.

Julie remembered what it had looked like back then and how hard the boys had worked on it.

They had extended and updated the kitchen, as well as adding a pool bathroom with a shower on the gulf-side of the property. A second-floor loft over the extension was built to serve as Marc's studio. It had its own small deck and stairs leading down to the pool

Julie usually felt queasy looking out on large expanses of water, but the view from Marc's studio didn't bother her…perhaps because of the lot in between. With its magnificent light and panorama, the loft had enabled and inspired Marc to paint a whole series of glorious sunsets.

All the decorating of the house had been left to David's artistic touch.

The kitchen, of course, was a chef's delight with the latest stainless steel appliances and gadgets. A low granite bar, surrounded by comfortable chairs, separated the cooking and dining areas. Rich teak leant its warmth to both the kitchen cabinets and the dining room table. Clean, white woodwork framed the windows and doors. In the living room, an exquisite oriental rug covered the stone-tiled floor, where tan suede couches beckoned, red pillows scattered here and there.

The neutral colors provided a perfect background for Marc's riotously colorful paintings, artfully placed around the house with gallery lighting.

Julie's gaze automatically went to the artwork, entranced by Marc's genius.

David spoke, snapping her out of it.

"Why don't you get yourself settled in, Julie, while I get us some refreshments. What would you like to drink? A nice, cold Chardonnay?"

"I'd love some, David. Thank you."

Julie pulled the carry-on bag behind her into the first bedroom on her left, where she usually stayed. She noticed that the big bed in the room at the end of the hallway was stripped of linens and personal things. Since Marc's diagnosis, David had been sleeping there. *He must have moved into Marc's room,* she thought.

The master bedroom and the studio loft were on the other end of the house. Julie recalled the times when Marc, in the grip of his muse, would climb the stairs and paint all through the night.

She closed her eyes tight, his presence palpable. It was hard to be in this room, in this house!

Sorely in need of comfort, Julie suddenly missed Joe Garrett.

The thought took her by surprise.

33

Julie sat in a comfortable swivel chair at the kitchen bar, admiring David's expertise as he prepared dinner. They were sharing some Brie and crackers and sipping Chardonnay, when she commented on the wine. David sat down next to her, took a sip, and began explaining the process that produced such a smooth, buttery taste.

Julie had no doubts about David but, now that he was sitting down instead of moving confidently around the kitchen, she couldn't help noticing some classic signs of concealment.

David's ankles were locked tight, even though he was passionate about wine and loved talking about it. He was markedly less animated …except for one odd gesture: He kept raising his hand to his mouth, like someone plagued with dental problems or shyness…neither of which applied.

Julie decided that he was literally "holding his tongue". There was something he was afraid to talk about.

"David, why didn't you tell me about Holiday Cruise Lines offer to buy the island?" she asked.

"Castle Cay? Why?" A puzzled frown settled on his face. "I don't have anything to do with the island. I've never even been there. What does that have to do with me? Especially now?"

Well, that's not his big secret, thought Julie. She couldn't help smiling. *I hope you don't play poker, David.*

"I don't know," she said, her mind returning to the sale. "It's just a lot of money…and because the sale coincides with Marc's death. Didn't you think it was odd?"

"No, I didn't, really," he said. "Marc wanted to sell it. He said that no one ever used it." His expression turned sympathetic.

"Marc told me what happened to you there, Julie. I felt so bad when I heard it; that was a horrible thing."

"Yes. It was," she said, pausing. "Neither of us had any reason to like the place. I was surprised when I heard the two of you were planning a trip there."

"So…you didn't go."

"No. Marc wanted to see the island again before it was sold. He wanted me to see it, too, but we never had the chance."

"I'm sorry, David. I know how terribly you miss him. I do, too."

David set down his wine glass, leaned over and hugged her.

"It's hard to be alone," he said. "I'm so glad you're here."

He was a sweet man. Julie wished he would confide in her.

The doorbell rang.

"That must be Rolly. I invited him for dinner."

"I'll get it," said Julie, going to the door.

Rolly Archer was a handsome guy with brown hair that brushed his collar, a little taller and more muscular than David. He wore a rose-colored silk shirt, pale linen slacks and boat shoes. He looked like a model, the clothes hanging comfortably on his frame.

"Hi, Rolly. C'mon in," she said. "David's up to his old tricks in the kitchen."

But David was out of the kitchen. He met Rolly halfway there and tearfully hugged him tight.

David's eyes briefly caught hers.

"Come sit down, I'll get you a glass of wine," he said quickly to Rolly, leading the way over to the bar.

The three of them stayed seated there for an informal dinner. In tacit agreement, they didn't mention Marc's death during their meal. Instead, they talked about the breezy weather, the local art scene and the Sandpiper Gallery, which was owned by Marc and his agent, Susan Dwyer.

Julie noted that the guarded behavior David had displayed earlier had disappeared in Rolly's company. Instead, he was subtly preening: tugging at his collar one minute and running his hands through his hair the next.

So that was your secret, David, thought Julie. *Rolly is your lover. For how long, I wonder?*

They were enjoying the strawberry shortcake when the doorbell rang. David went to answer it.

Suddenly, he was confronted with video cameras and police.

"David Harris? You're under arrest for the murder of Marcus Solomon."

34

"Julie!"

David's eyes searched frantically for her, as the police handcuffed him.

Julie dug in her purse, and found the scrap of paper on which she had scribbled a name and number.

Jacob Goldman (305) 438-5253

She ran out the door, Rolly right behind her. "Don't worry, David!" she yelled to him as they ducked him into the back of the cruiser. She waved the paper. "I'll get Jake Goldman! We'll be there soon!"

The cruiser pulled away with David looking back at her, a picture of distress.

Brushing past Rolly, Julie ran back in the house and grabbed the phone. Hurriedly, she punched in the number.

"Goldman Law Firm," a woman's voice said. "Can you hold, please?"

"*No*, I can't! I need to speak to Jacob Goldman right away! Tell him David Harris has just been charged with murdering Marc Solomon!"

"And who am I speaking to, please?"

"My name is Julie O'Hara, and I'm calling about *David Harris*."

"Just a moment, please," the woman said in a maddeningly calm voice. And then Julie was on hold…waiting and waiting.

"I better go, Julie," said Rolly. "I'll call you later."

Julie nodded, still on hold, listening to inane music. Suddenly, it ended. "Hello, this is Jake Goldman," said a deep, authoritative voice.

"Mr. Goldman! I'm Julie O'Hara. I'm a friend of Joe Garrett in Orlando. He said for David Harris to call you if he needed an attorney. The police have just been here and arrested him for murder! Can you meet him at the Key West police station?"

"Yes. I'm just finishing with a client. But I'm in Key Largo, near Miami, Ms. O'Hara…it'll take me a couple hours to get there."

"Thank you so much," she said. "I'm going there now. I'll tell David."

Julie saw the keys to the VW on the kitchen counter. She snatched them up, along with her purse, and ran out the front door. There were some neighbors outside who had just witnessed poor David's ignominy. Julie asked one of the men if he knew where the police station was located. He gave her directions, and she thanked him and took off.

When she got there, reporters were milling around outside. It looked like they were setting up for a press conference. She went inside the crowded station and up to the desk. Explaining who she was, she asked to see David.

"Sorry, Miss. Not right now. You can wait out here if you want."

"But I want to let him know that his lawyer is on the way," she said.

"When his lawyer gets here, he can go in. Sorry."

Julie knew there was nothing she could do.

"Officer? Do you happen to know the attorney, Jacob Goldman?"

"Yeah, I know Jake Goldman."

"He'll be here in about two hours," she said. "I plan to be back here waiting for him, but I've never met him. Will you point him out to me when he comes in?"

"Sure."

Julie drove directly to the nearest bar with a TV, and ordered a scotch and soda. Sure enough, at the top of the hour, David's arrest was on the local news channel. She sat there, astonished at the suddenness of the police department's action. Apparently, they felt they had enough circumstantial evidence to move forward with a murder charge!

She shook her head, knowing that David had no alibi.

Jake Goldman arrived about an hour after Julie came back from the bar, and the officer signaled her up to the desk. The attorney appeared to be in his fifties with hair like steel wool and dark rimmed glasses. He'd set his briefcase on the floor and was talking to the officer when Julie walked up.

"Mr. Goldman, I'm Julie O'Hara. I called you."

"It's Jake. Nice to meet you, Julie," he said, shaking her hand. "It's a good thing you did. I better get in there. No point in you waiting here. He'll be here at least overnight. I'll tell him you were here. He should be able to call you."

And with that, he was gone. The man's brisk, all-business manner was reassuring; he wasn't wasting any time. Julie made her way out through the crowd, and went back to the house to wait for David's call.

It was 10:00 pm when he finally did.

"Julie, it's David."

He sounded tired, beaten down.

She hit the mute button on the TV remote.

"David! I'm so glad to hear from you! I tried to get in to see you," she said. "Have you seen Jake Goldman?"

"Yes, thank God. Thank you for calling him. An arraignment is scheduled for tomorrow morning. Jake said that 'I shouldn't worry'. *As if!* Anyway, he expects that I'll get bail, because I have no record and long ties to the community."

"Should I be there to pick you up?"

"No. Jake said once bail is arranged, the police will

take me home. They'll make me wear an electronic ankle cuff." He sighed.

"This is a *nightmare*, Julie."

"I know. But Jake's right, don't worry," said Julie. "Do you know Joe Garrett, the private investigator in my office building? He's helping you, too, David. He's following up on a lead right now! And Jake Goldman has an *excellent* reputation. You're in good hands...and I'll stay right here at the house with you.

"Their case has to be flimsy, David. They can't prove it, because they've got the *wrong* man. It's going to be all right. I'll be waiting here for you when you get home."

"Thank you, Julie. I'm so grateful. I have to hang up now, bye."

Julie wished that her confidence would catch up with her acting.

At midnight, she went to bed, sick of the hyper television coverage.

Julie tossed and turned, checking the illuminated clock every half hour.

She was desperate to get some sleep! At two o'clock, in the soft light from the pool patio, she crossed the house to the master bedroom. She went to the medicine cabinet in the adjoining bath to look for something to help her sleep.

Fortunately, David had a prescription for Xanax and she took one.

Julie shuffled back through the silent house to the guest room, climbed into bed and was soon fast asleep.

She never noticed the date on the prescription.

35

I s that my cell phone ringing?
Julie stumbled out of bed, fished around in her purse, and pulled out the phone. It was too late. She checked the caller ID.

Area code 305? Isn't that Miami?

Half asleep, she called the number. It rang just once.

"Hello?" a familiar voice said.

"This is Julie O'Hara," she said.

"Merlin! It's Joe!"

"Hi…Are you in Miami?"

"Yes. I'm at Will Sawyer's house. We're flying to Castle Cay this morning. We're just heading for the airport now. I saw the news about David's arrest on TV! What's happening?"

"I don't know any more than you do, Joe." said Julie. "I did meet Jake Goldman, though. He seems like a good attorney. Poor David is beside himself with worry. I'm hoping he'll be out on bail later today."

"I hope so, too," he said. "Did you say that there's a caretaker on Castle Cay?"

"Yes. John Drum. His wife's name is Mary...and there's a boy, Alfred."

"Okay. We'll get some aerial shots and I'll try to talk to him," he said. "I've got to go, Merlin. Will's waiting for me. Be sure you tell Jake Goldman about the island, and Holiday's offer to buy it. A deal that big...it's hard to imagine it's not connected. Gotta go. I'll call you when I get back. "

They hung up, and Julie thought about all the people and events cropping up in her investigation. She showered and dressed quickly. Then she put on a pot of coffee, and went up to Marc's studio.

The loft had large, sliding windows all around. Outside, the storm shutters were lifted high, cranked fully open. The view of the Gulf was spectacular. An unfinished canvas was on the easel, and Marc's voice echoed faintly... *"I love the sunset after a storm..."* Julie inhaled sharply, closed her eyes and turned away from the painting.

Finished canvases were stacked, one after another, on a rack in the right corner of the room. A counter ran along two of the walls, just under the windows. Art supplies filled the shelves below: canvas and wood, smooth boards, pads, papers, palettes, etc. On the top, more supplies: oil and acrylic paints, watercolor paints, brushes of every size and shape...and cans, cans, everywhere.

Julie saw the items she had come up for: a large,

white sheet of heavy paper, a fat pencil and a roll of masking tape. She brought them all downstairs, and taped the sheet of paper to the refrigerator.

There. Now I'm going to organize this...

The phone rang. It was Rolly, worried about David.

Julie told him that she didn't know anything that wasn't on the news, except that she expected David to be out on bail later in the day. Rolly asked her to have David call him as soon as he could.

Were they lovers when Marc was alive?

The phone rang again.

It was David's mother in Illinois. She was hysterical. Julie explained who she was, and told her David's arrest was a terrible mistake, that he would be home later today, and that she shouldn't worry….and yes, of course, she would have him call her right away.

She hung up again.

And the phone rang again!

The Caller ID said, "Key West Citizen", a local newspaper.

This time Julie didn't pick it up.

She began her chart.

I'm going to assume David is innocent, in spite of his relationship with Rolly. I have to find out how long that's been going on. Still, I don't think it matters. David is grieving for Marc.

So…if there was no forced entry, and no one but Marc and David had a key…then Marc had to let someone in, right? Someone he knew.

Oh, God. That could be anybody! Never mind, I'll put in what I know.

Julie listed the few names she had: Avram Solomon, Frank Martino, Rolly Archer and Susan Dwyer.

In her own shorthand, she filled in everything she knew about them, including events and possible connections: The Solomon auto dealerships, the sale of Castle Cay, the Sandpiper Art Gallery and Marc's Boston show.

Meanwhile, the phone kept on ringing.

Around noontime, David came home.

36

J ulie had never seen David looking like this, so tired, red-eyed and disheveled. She hugged him and led him to one of the comfortable kitchen chairs.

"I was just about to make a BLT and have a glass of Chardonnay. Want some?" she asked.

"Oh, yes, please," he said, "especially the Chardonnay."

"David, your mother called, and Rolly called, too. They both want you to call them as soon as possible. They're worried about you."

"I'm so tired," he said. "But I'll call them right after lunch. I'm just glad to be home. It was so *terrible* in there…" He started to cry. "I miss Marc so much."

Julie pushed the napkin holder toward him; he took one and wiped his eyes. She understood what it was like to suddenly lose someone you loved so much. But, she couldn't imagine being humiliated and thrown in jail on top of it.

Like kicking a hit-and-run victim.

When David looked up, he noticed the big chart taped to the refrigerator.

"What's that?" he asked.

Julie poured them a glass of wine and began preparing the sandwiches.

"Somebody killed Marc, David...and it wasn't you. Joe and I are collecting a lot of information right now, and I'm organizing it," she said, putting a plate of bacon in the microwave.

"What can I do to help?" he said.

"Well, we need to talk some more about some of these people, and maybe some others. Right now, though, I think you need to get some sleep."

"You're right. I haven't slept at all since they took me in yesterday,' he said. "After we eat, I'll call my mother and I'll call Rolly. Maybe he can come over tomorrow and help us, too." He sighed. "After that, I think I will go to bed."

It seemed like an opportune time to let him know that she was aware of their relationship.

"David, I know about Rolly."

He set his wine down, shocked.

"He *told* you?"

Without waiting for a response, David rushed on. "He didn't do it, Julie! He never left my side; I would have known! He was just as shocked as I was!"

Julie closed her mouth, which had fallen open.

Rolly Archer stayed here that night. That's what David was hiding.

"Why didn't you tell the police Rolly was here, that you found Marc *together*?"

"Didn't he tell you?" he said, confused.

"David. Rolly never told me anything. I guessed that you two were on intimate terms with each other. *That's all I meant.*"

"Oh, God," he said, his hand covering his mouth. It was much too late, as the truth had already escaped like a canary from an opened cage.

37

Below the helicopter, the Caribbean Sea was a sparkling vision of blue and green shades, from pale aqua to emerald. There were white caps here and there, rippling across the surface, and they were flying low enough to clearly see the fishing boats and pleasure craft.

"There, Joe, look!" yelled Will. "Check the map, northeast!"

Joe could barely hear Will over the sound of the rotor blades. He adjusted his headphones, cupping his ears more securely. They were passing over a very large, crescent shaped island, which encircled an innumerable amount of small isles to its left. It was very developed, lots of pastel stucco homes.

"Not here. Ahead of us, to the left," said Will.

Joe could hear him better now.

"The small outer islands in a string, running north and south. See that one with all the boats and buildings? That's Green Turtle Cay. Just past it…there's Manjack …mostly empty. Do you see it?"

Joe was following the names on the map and looking in the direction Will was pointing. He saw the island named Manjack Cay, and nodded.

"Okay," Will said, "There's Castle Cay, straight ahead of us, northeast of Manjack. It's the furthest out-island. See it?"

"Yes, I do," said Joe.

The island was shaped like an elongated triangle from north to south. The western side of Castle Cay, which they were approaching, stuck out toward them in a wide V shape. There was a picture-perfect beach ringed with palm trees to the right of the V point, and a long boat dock. A house sat up high in the dense foliage.

The chopper climbed, scaling a high, rocky ridge that ran the length of Castle Cay. As they cleared the top, a broad terrace appeared below, dropping off to a long, nearly straight edge sliced against the deep, cobalt blue ocean.

"Well, buddy," said Will, pointing. "You're in luck! There's an airstrip over there. We can land, if you want."

"Can we get some pictures of the island first and then come back and land here?" asked Joe.

"Sure. The camera's all set to go. Hang on, while I circle the place."

There were a couple of small buildings near the airstrip, and a rock/cement wall and pier. Joe could see the waves, rolling against the land in a long, jagged line of white foam. As they flew south, he noticed a small indentation, a beach, protected by a reef. The far southern end of the island tapered off into a string of shoals.

As they came back, heading north up the Caribbean side on the west, there was a great deal more foliage. They passed the ridge house again. It was shuttered and deserted, a blind sentinel above a gorgeous beach. The long dock stretched out over shallows so clear they could see schools of fish.

"Even you could catch one here, old buddy," said Will.

Joe laughed, shaking his head.

Ahead, around the bend, they saw what looked like an old farmhouse. There was a barn and some ramshackle buildings, with no one in sight. They continued on, but saw no other houses or structures. Castle Cay's big central ridge led to smaller, empty islands on its northern tip trailing like a rocky green spine on a partially submerged alligator. They banked to the right and headed south once more on the far side of the high ridge.

The chopper lowered, gently swinging from side to side, and settled on the cracked landing strip. They got out and walked toward the cement block structures. There was nothing much inside: one had a long, portable wooden table that was damaged and falling apart, and there was some debris...pieces of plastic wrap, paper, a soda can.

"Drug runners," said Joe.

"Yeah, sure looks like it, buddy. I saw another empty island with a makeshift strip like this in the southern Bahamas. I was flying a narc. He was looking for it. He said they usually just did drops. But, you know that big ridge there? You can't see this set-up from the other side of this island."

"Looks like it hasn't been used for awhile," said Joe.

"No," said Will. "You say Holiday Cruise Line is interested in this place?"

"Oh, yeah. Forty million interested."

"That would be a hell of a deal for them, Joe. The water's deep on this side; they could bring a ship in close. Plus they already have a sea wall and a pier for the tenders."

"Yeah. And it's not too wide for them to cut through to that beautiful beach on the other side."

"Was there supposed to be a 'caretaker' or somebody living on this island?"

"That's what Julie told me. But those houses we passed on the other side are abandoned...probably scared off by the drug runners."

"Hey...there's an airport on Treasure Cay," said Will. "We're passing right over it on our way back. We could land and ask around about Castle Cay. A lot of these Bahamians, particularly the fishing boats, they know everything about these islands."

"That would be great. Let's do it."

They climbed aboard, Will revved up the chopper and they lifted off...leaving the shadowy ghosts of Castle Cay behind.

They left the chopper at the airport on Treasure Cay. While they waited for a cab, Joe picked up a brochure featuring four fishing boats and their captains:

- *FISH ABACOS* -
Half Day or Full Day

Excitedly, he showed it to Will on the way to the marina.

"Look at this guy, Will. '*Captain Al Drum*'. He's got the same name as the caretaker Julie mentioned. She said his name was 'John Drum' and I think she said there was a son, 'Alfred'. I bet it's him. Here's his boat, *Wave Dancer II.* Let's see if we can find him."

It was two in the afternoon when they located *Wave Dancer*'s slip.

"She'll be back about four," said a teenage boy washing down a catamaran moored nearby. "Al had four guys, an all day charter."

They thanked him, and decided to go grab some lunch at the Marina Bar & Grill and return a little later.

They took a seat in the restaurant and both ordered 'Fish N' Chips' and Cokes. When the waitress walked away, Will grinned at Joe.

"Well, you sure have gotten yourself a case, Joe."

"Yeah, it's a puzzle, all right."

"I meant a case of the hots for Merlin," said Will.

"Yeah," said Joe, smiling, "that, too."

At half past three, they were sitting on a wooden bench on the dock waiting for *WaveDancer II.* She pulled in neatly, right on schedule. One by one, four sunburned, happy guys shook Captain Al's hand and left. The Captain himself was dark haired and medium height, late twenties, maybe thirty. He was deeply tanned, as was his mate, a blond fellow about the same age. They started to clean up the boat.

"Excuse me," said Joe, "Alfred Drum?"

"Al," he said. "Yeah, that's me. Can I help you?"

"I wonder if your father is John Drum, who used to be the caretaker out on Castle Cay?"

"Why do you want to know?"

Joe introduced himself and Will, and explained that the owner of the island, Marc Solomon, had died under suspicious circumstances. He told him that Julie O'Hara - a close friend of Mr. Solomon - had hired him to investigate the man's death. Joe pulled out his wallet and gave him one of his business cards.

"Yes, I'm John Drum's son," said Al. "I used to live on Castle Cay. I'm sorry to hear about Marc Solomon. I haven't seen him in years, but he was a nice guy. And I'll never forget Julie O'Hara, even though she only came to Castle Cay once. What would you like to know?"

"When did your family leave Castle Cay?"

"In 1994," said Al. "Mrs. Solomon had a heart attack while they were on vacation there in '93. I think they kind of thought the island was cursed or something after that. Anyway, the family said they didn't need us there anymore. They gave my father a nice severance and we moved here. I have to tell you, my mother and I didn't mind. It was a lonely life out there."

"So, do you ever go back?"

"No, never have. There were rumors about men with rifles on the island. I never went near Castle Cay after I heard that. There's still pirates out here that'll steal your equipment, or your whole boat. You got to be careful, you know?"

"Yeah, I guess you do," said Joe. "One other thing, Al. You mentioned that Julie O'Hara came here once. When was that? Was she with Marc Solomon?"

Al Drum looked at him, surprised.

"No. She was with Dan O'Hara on her honeymoon. He died there…you don't know about that?"

38

Special Agent Sherman Dixon had gotten the call from the Executive Assistant Director's office in Washington, D.C. Thomas Wright, EAD, wanted to meet with him. Sherm had no idea what it was about when he walked in and sat down, but he found out fast.

"Good morning, Agent Dixon. Have a seat."

"Good morning, sir," said Sherm.

"I'd like you to explain what you know about a man named Avram Solomon and why you inquired about him," said the EAD.

Uh-oh...

"I went to college with a guy, Joe Garrett, who is a private investigator now. We were talking on the phone about his girlfriend, who's originally from Boston," said Sherm. "She was a good friend of Marcus Solomon. You recall that artist who was murdered in Key West, sir?"

"Oh, yes."

"Well, she mentioned to my friend that she was suspicious of the victim's brother, Avram Solomon.

She told Joe she knew some people who worked for this Solomon guy in Boston, who thought he might be doing something illegal with his car dealership business," said Sherm.

"Some people? Who?"

"I don't know their names, sir. I asked about this Solomon guy out of curiosity. I thought he might be laundering money, maybe, for the Tambini family. But no one recognized the name and he wasn't in the system. Sir? May I ask what this is about?"

"Yes, you may. You are being temporarily assigned to a Top Secret task force in Boston. It's an ongoing drug investigation. This individual, Avram Solomon, has recently figured into it.

"You are to gather as much information as you can from your friend, the detective, and his girlfriend, too…especially the names of any people who work for, or with Solomon, and who might have pertinent information that they are willing to share with us.

"Then you are to fly immediately to Boston to meet Special Agent in Charge, Robert Branson, who is heading up this task force," said the EAD. "And, Agent Dixon, you can't tell anyone about this investigation. You have to get this information without divulging anything about the task force. Is that clear?"

"Yes, sir."

"Good. I don't want any leaks from this office."

"No, sir."

"All right, then. Good luck to you," he said, extending his hand.

"Thank you, sir," said Sherm, giving his hand a final shake. "Goodbye."

Sounds like Joe's suspect is up to his eyeballs in illegal activities, thought Sherm, as he walked down the hall toward the elevator. *But how the hell does it connect with the brother's death in Key West?*

39

As exhausted as David was, it might have been kinder to just let him go to bed. But Julie knew that she had a better chance of getting the whole story out of him now…and, besides, she was angry with him.

"Why did you lie about Rolly being here when you found Marc?"

"I didn't lie, Julie. Nobody asked me," he said.

"What?" she said. "You told the police that Rolly left when Susan left!"

"Well, he did. They never asked me if he came back."

"I don't believe this! You're charged with murder, and you're protecting Rolly? What are you doing with him, anyway? I don't understand how you could do that to Marc."

"That's why we didn't tell the police!" said David, standing up now, pacing back and forth. "They wouldn't understand, either. Marc knew all about Rolly and me. He didn't mind, Julie! Marc and I loved each other, but we haven't had a sexual relationship for years."

"How do you know that Rolly didn't kill Marc?"

"I know. He couldn't. He wouldn't."

There was no point arguing with him. *He'll be more rational after he gets some sleep. In any case, Jake Goldman needs to know about this.*

After David went to bed, Julie added to the chart, under Rolly Archer.

Had opportunity. Jealousy? Money? Any connection to Avram Solomon?

She had set the phone's ringer on Low. It rang periodically throughout the afternoon. She answered it twice. The first time was when the Caller ID read, 'Jacob Goldman'. He asked to speak to David.

"He's sleeping, Jake. This is Julie. I'll wake him if you want me to, but he was really wiped out and upset. He may have taken a sleeping pill."

"Yes, I know. Unfortunately, so do the police, who found a lot of alprazolam in the deceased."

Alprazolam…generic for Xanax?

"So, Julie, you seem to really care for David. How long have you known him?"

"I was Marc Solomon's friend for eighteen years. I've been David's friend since he met Marc, many years ago. And, of course, I believe he's innocent."

"I think he probably is, too. But I get the feeling he's holding back something," he said. "Do you have any idea what that might be?"

"Yes, I do. But I think David should tell you himself," she said.

"Jake, I'm a body language specialist. I've been a jury consultant on two murder cases. If there's anything I can do to help, I'm here. And you know Joe Garrett; he's following another lead we think is related to Marc's murder. We hope to find evidence that will exonerate David, at least provide reasonable doubt."

"I'm coming over there tomorrow morning to meet with David, about ten. Will you be there? And can you have Joe there, too?"

"Yes. I expect him this evening."

"Well, I'm all ears, Julie. I'll see you in the morning, then."

Julie hung up and thought about the sleeping pills. *The damn bottle was new, not the prescription. Why else would it be significant to the DA? I'll check it later. Still…couldn't Marc have been prescribed the same drug? No, probably not; they have to know his medications.*

She took the chart down, took it to her room and slipped it under the bed.

David kept on sleeping.

The second time she answered the phone, it was Joe.

"Hi! How did the trip to Castle Cay go?" asked Julie, suddenly aware of how much the damn place was on her mind these days.

"It went fine, Merlin. I've got a lot to tell you. Will's flying me to Key West now. I was hoping you could pick me up, or should I rent a car and check in somewhere?"

"No! I mean...no, don't rent a car. I'll pick you up. David's asleep, probably for the night. We could stop somewhere for dinner. I haven't eaten, have you?"

Joe gave her the time and place, and Julie hung up.

It only makes sense for him to stay here. There is an empty bedroom, after all.

40

The wind over the Caribbean was chasing its own tail southeast of Cuba, but Key West was getting a typical, late-day thunderstorm, albeit a windy one. It was almost eight and Julie and Joe were so hungry, they decided not to wait out the downpour. They jumped out of the VW and ran into the Rusty Pelican.

The restaurant was cozy, decorated in a nautical motif. Dimly lit ship's lanterns reflected on polished wood, and matching hurricane candles sat on each table. They requested a booth and were seated right away. Julie picked up a napkin and used it to dab at her wet face and dripping hair.

"You look good wet," said Joe.

Suddenly Julie's face grew warm.

I'm blushing! What am I, a teenager?

Anxious to redirect his attention, she asked, "So how was the flight in this terrible weather?"

"Nice segue," said Joe, laughing. "Truth? It was tough. The nearer we got to Key West, the more the wind and rain played havoc with the chopper. Will was as miserable as a cat in a tub...and he took off just about as fast."

They were seated in the bar side of the restaurant, and the young bartender came over and took their food and drink order. Julie ordered a chardonnay, and Joe an iced tea. She noticed that there were a few men seated at the bar who were watching ESPN. Fortunately, the sound was turned down.

It didn't take long for the young man to serve their drinks.

"I found out something important from David," Julie said, taking a sip.

"What?"

"The night of the murder, Marc and David had two dinner guests, Rolly Archer, a friend of theirs, and Susan Dwyer, Marc's agent. They left together at ten-thirty. In a weak moment this afternoon, David told me that Rolly came back later and they spent the whole night together. He said they found Marc's body *together*."

"Holy shit! He hasn't told the police that?"

"No. I think he's in love with Rolly."

"That guy could have done it!" said Joe.

"That's what I said. David refuses to consider the possibility. He said he 'knows Rolly never left his side'."

"He's got to tell the cops, Julie."

She nodded. "He's going to tell Jake Goldman in the morning."

"It's going to make him look guilty as hell, you know."

"Yeah, I know," she said, sighing in resignation. "Tell me about your trip to Castle Cay."

"Well, I think there's been some changes since you were there…"

Joe proceeded to tell her everything; everything except for Al Drum's recounting of her honeymoon ordeal, which had pierced Joe's heart and explained a lot. He hoped that Julie, herself, would decide to share that with him. In any case, this certainly wasn't the time to bring it up.

"Anyhow, Merlin, the airstrip and the cement block buildings…there's no doubt they were built by drug traffickers. And the caretaker, John Drum, was fired in 1994 by the Solomon family."

"The Solomon *family*? That had to mean Avram," said Julie. "Marc's mother died on Castle Cay in 1993. According to her brother, none of the family went there after that. I know Marc never did…plus, it was in the trust, which was managed by Avram! Do you think he knew about the drugs?"

"Maybe. Maybe that ties into your suspicions about his business, too."

"I wouldn't be surprised! I think Avram is a pathological liar, Joe. Matt Castle thinks so, too, and he's known him all his life. I'm also sure that Avram *hated* Marc. But he has an airtight alibi; he was definitely in Boston. And damn it, I just can't see what he would gain from selling the island, since the proceeds don't even go to him."

"So the sale is done?" asked Joe.

"No. Pending, I think. I met with the agent at Island World Realty in Miami who's handling the sale. His name is Frank Martino. He stands to make a serious commission. He's the listing *and* selling agent," she added.

"Miami isn't far from here, Julie."

"Yeah, I was thinking that, too," she said. "Also, I suspect that Marc never signed the sales agreement. Martino thought I was a real estate agent and he made a point of telling me that Avram, as trustee, could sign the deal."

"So you think that Marc didn't want to sell?"

"That's the weird part, Joe. From all accounts, he *did* want to sell."

The two of them, stymied, suspended conversation for a while and dug into their broiled grouper.

Julie put down her fork and looked up.

"I was thinking, Joe…Jake Goldman is coming tomorrow morning to see David. I told him that you were working with me on this, and he asked to see the two of us, as well. Why don't you stay at the house?" She hastened to add, "There*'s* an extra bedroom…"

"I thought you'd never ask."

Julie smiled along with him…for the first time.

They looked outside and decided to wait a little longer to see if the rain might let up. Over coffee, their conversation turned to other subjects…life in Orlando…the weather.

The bartender had raised the volume, and they turned toward the television. On screen, a weather channel reporter was talking about tropical storm Carlo and the deluge it was dumping in Haiti.

It was ten-thirty by the time they arrived at David's house. Julie had left very few lights on and she surmised that David was still asleep because it was still dark inside. As she closed the front door behind them, she flipped on the gallery-light switch illuminating the paintings all around the walls.

"Wow!" said Joe, transfixed.

"I know. Aren't they beautiful?"

"They're the essence of Key West…the way it *feels*."

Julie was surprised at Joe's succinct appreciation of Marc's art. *There's more to him than meets the eye.*

"I'll show you his studio in the morning, Joe. You really can't appreciate it at night. You must be tired; I know I am."

She turned right into the hallway, leading the way to the bedroom at the end, which she had made up for him earlier. But she didn't walk into it. Instead, she stood awkwardly in the narrow hallway, sort of ushering him in. "The bathroom is over there," she said, "and my room is over here."

I can't believe I said that!

Joe looked at her with his eyebrows raised and a slight smile, his eyes dropping to her mouth and then rising back up to her eyes. He squeezed past her.

"Well, then...goodnight," he said, as he closed his door.

"Yes, goodnight."

Julie bit her lip softly, unconsciously.

Definitely more to him...

41

Guy Tambini was at his father's house in Newton, Massachusetts, just west of Boston. He was very uncomfortable; he didn't like being reprimanded by his father, Silvio, especially in front of one of his men. It was humiliating, and it was all because of that prick, Avram Solomon.

The family had certain cops and FBI agents who kept them informed about things. Avram Solomon's name had come up in an FBI meeting. Apparently, an agent named "Dixon" was asking if anyone "had anything" on Solomon.

"So? They don't have anything on him," said Guy.

"Yeah? They will, if they start looking," said Silvio.

Guy had first met with Avram Solomon in 1994 to talk about Castle Cay, and he had to admit that the arrogant bastard had balls. Avram had heard about the construction activity on the eastern side of the island from Drum, the caretaker. He'd immediately gone to the island and headed for the site on horseback.

Of course, Guy's armed guards stopped him.

Avram blew a gasket.

"I own the fucking place", he said and demanded to be taken to the person in charge. As if he was in a position to demand anything, surrounded by guys holding rifles! But his audacity worked. They led him to Joey Tedesco, who was overseeing things.

Avram never even got off his horse.

"You tell your boss that I want to meet him in Boston. My family owns this fucking island, and I'm ready to make things a lot easier for him."

With that, he'd handed Joey a piece of paper with his name and phone number, wheeled his horse around and left... unimpeded.

Guy had set up a meeting with him right afterwards. It was agreed that Avram would get a piece of the action for getting rid of the caretaker, and for allowing the Tambini family unfettered and unreported use of Castle Cay.

By 2006, the Caribbean had gotten too hot, what with Homeland Security and the Bahamian government cooperating with the Feds. They'd shut the route down. It was easier to get the drugs in over the Mexico-California border.

They were still dealing with Avram Solomon, though. They stored the stuff in an old, closed up gas station on a corner lot owned by him, next to Solomon's Boston store. There was also a lab built into the back of a warehouse surrounded by woods, behind a storage lot Solomon owned in Waltham.

It was worth it to the Tambini family not to have these places in their name. Avram Solomon had balls of steel and no scruples…and they paid him well for it. But he was a greedy bastard…too greedy for his own good.

"You let Solomon know that he better keep a low profile if he wants to keep our business," said Silvio in quiet voice that no one took lightly.

Avram was on the phone for some time, reassuring Guy Tambini that there was "nothing to worry about". When he was finally able to hang up, he was thoroughly irked. He knew that, somehow, the inquiry at the FBI had originated with that bitch, Julie O'Hara.

First, there was the problem of his brother deciding out of the blue to visit Castle Cay…and now this!

I need to dump that fucking island. Why couldn't the fag just sign the papers? Forty fucking million? This should have been so simple!

The cruise line had no interest in Castle Cay's history, other than the Blackbeard legend. They planned to build over everything, to convert the island into a pirate-themed port. From Avram's view, that would physically and psychologically erase the island's connection to drug trafficking…and to himself.

At least the Keystone Kops arrested David Harris. I wish him a speedy trial.

42

J ulie awoke to a soft tapping on her bedroom door.
"Julie? It's me…David."

"Hmm, c'mon in," she said.

David entered, closing the door behind him, and sat on the wicker chair near the bed. He was wearing light khaki shorts and a matching shirt. His blond hair was parted in the middle and it fell on either side of his face. With the electronic ankle cuff on, Julie thought he looked like a forlorn cocker spaniel with his collar in the wrong place.

"I'm sorry, Julie," he said. "I know it was lousy of me to lie to you about Rolly. We knew it didn't look good, our being together; and we *both* thought Marc had killed himself."

"It's all right, David, people do strange things under stress. But you have to tell your lawyer, you know. By the way, Jake called while you were sleeping yesterday. He's coming over this morning about ten. What time is it? "

"It's eight o'clock," he said.

"I better get dressed," she said, getting out of bed. "Oh, did you get my note about Joe Garrett staying here? I hope that's okay?"

"Oh, yes. It's fine. He's already up. Listen...there's something else I didn't tell you, Julie. About Rolly. He was convicted on a drug charge, 'possession', and he's on probation. That was another reason that we didn't want to say that he was here."

"Drugs? What kind of a person is he? What do you really know about this guy, David?"

"It was only marijuana, and he didn't even buy it for himself!"

Oh, my God. Naïve doesn't begin to describe you, thought Julie. Holding her tongue, she said, "Well, whatever he is, you've got to tell Jake Goldman."

"I know," he said. "I called Rolly this morning and told him I was going to do that. I felt it was only fair to warn him."

Brilliant.

"Hmm. Well, let me get dressed before Jake gets here," she said.

David left, and Julie sat for a moment just shaking her head in bewilderment. His innocence and trust were truly amazing.

It would have made it easy for Rolly...

Julie got up and took a quick shower. Afterwards, she put on some shorts and a tee shirt and joined David and Joe in the kitchen. The French doors facing the water were open, and a warm breeze filled the house with fresh, salty air. She noticed that there were a few clouds but, for the most part, it was sunny.

"Good morning, Joe."

He had the thermal coffee pot in one hand and three mugs in the other.

"Morning, Merlin. The weather's calmed down; it's a nice day! David suggested that we have our breakfast out by the pool."

She saw that David was already there, placing things on the table.

"Well, this looks good!" she said, stepping outside. There was fresh fruit and juice, sliced ham and muffins.

"Help yourself," he said.

Joe poured each of them a cup of coffee.

"What a great spot this is, David. Are one of those yours?" he said smiling, indicating the two huge yachts at anchor across the canal.

"I *wish*," said David. "That's ours, over there on the right," he said pointing to a cigarette boat covered with canvas and secured to a lift. *Boyz Boat, Key West* was painted on the rear. "I'm glad it's up out of the water; it's pretty rough out there."

Julie had noticed that the yachts were rocking quite a bit.

"What's up with 'Carlo'? Anyone see the forecast?" she asked.

"It's stalled over Haiti and Jamaica," said Joe.

"They're getting inundated. They expect it to strengthen as it moves west."

"I hope it stays south of Cuba," said David. He held up his leg with the ankle cuff. "I'm not allowed to *e-vac-uate,"* he said, drawing out the word.

They all laughed.

Julie was glad to see David's droll, theatrical personality back in place. Perhaps it was a good time to ask him a question. "David, I was wondering...how did you meet Rolly?"

"I think we actually met at the Sandpiper. Yes, it was at the gallery, when he was here on a vacation. He's one of Susan's artists now. Marc knew him from Boston. They went to the same art school up there," he said.

From Boston...does he know Avram?

"Speaking of that," said David, "would you like to see the studio, Joe?"

"Sure," said Joe, setting down his coffee.

The phone rang just as they walked back inside and David picked it up.

"Hi! Yes, I'm fine...Oh, yes. I'd forgotten all about it, what with everything... Can I call you this afternoon? My attorney is coming over this morning. Okay, good...talk to you later. Bye."

"That was Susan," said David, as he led the way upstairs. "I completely forgot about Marc's New York show. She needs some more paintings. I'll have to let her come over today or tomorrow. She needs time for framing and shipping."

"They're still going ahead with the show?" said Julie.

"Oh, yes. There's a contract with Herzog Gallery in New York."

"What a view!" said Joe, stepping up into the loft.

"Yes, it is beautiful...*outside*," said David. "I don't have to tell you that the cleaning lady doesn't set foot up here. *I'm* even forbidden to touch anything." Sighing, he said, "Well, not *now*, I guess.

"Come on over here," he said, walking toward the finished canvases on the rack. "Here's some more of Marc's work."

Joe began to flip through them, admiring the canvases one at a time. There were some that Julie hadn't seen, too. It was easy to recognize Marc's style...the riotous colors, the bold brush strokes. There was a consistency, whether it was Key West storefronts and tourists, fishing boats or sunsets. At the end of the stack were two paintings that were clearly different from the rest. They were somber, done in shades of gray, from silver to black with deepening blues. Palms bent under dark clouds, and waves lashed the shore. Each had NFS - Not For Sale - on top of the canvas frame.

"Are these Marc's?" asked Joe.

"Yes," said Julie. "It's Castle Cay. He did them right after his mother died. That was Marc's last visit there, I believe," said Julie, pulling out the painting. "Yes. See here, under his signature? 1993."

"They're beautiful, haunting," said Joe, looking at Julie.

Does he know about Dan?

"Uh, let's go downstairs and finish our breakfast," said David.

Julie returned the painting to the stack. They followed David out the rear studio door to an open deck, which partially covered the master suite below. Descending the outside stairs to the pool patio, Julie noticed that the breeze had picked up and clouds were scudding by.

"Joe, maybe we should go to the Sandpiper Gallery today."

It was shortly after ten when Jake Goldman arrived. Julie opened the door to let him in. The wind gusting through the open doors across the room slammed the front door shut behind him. The two of them jumped, startled.

"Boy! That's some wind," said Jake. "I hope Carlo isn't turning our way."

Julie rushed to close the French doors, while David offered Jake some coffee. They all took a seat around the dining room table.

"All right now," said Jake, opening his briefcase, "Julie and Joe, I want to know everything that you two have discovered thus far that may possibly relate to this case.

"But first, David, I need to go over the whole sequence of events with you, and I want the complete truth. I'm going to take notes and also record this entire meeting. Of course, anything you tell me is confidential and we can turn off the recorder at any time, if you wish. Now, why don't you start with the dinner party you and Marc were hosting the night before he died."

This time David told the whole story, including Rolly's pretense of leaving with Susan and immediately returning. David stressed that they'd all consumed a lot of wine, and that both he and Rolly had slept soundly through the night. They had awakened with headaches. It was around nine o'clock and they had gotten up and started looking around for Marc. David said that he went into Marc's bedroom and found him, and that he'd called out to Rolly to come in. According to David they were "both totally shocked."

Julie could tell that Jake Goldman was used to clients lying to him; he didn't seem fazed by David's latest account of the truth. But he did look puzzled.

"Why didn't you both stay there and wait for the police? Why did you cover for this man, Rolly, or Roland Archer?" asked Jake, clarifying the name for the tape.

David explained about their affair being secret, and about Rolly being on probation.

"David, do you realize that Rolly may have lied to you, that he may be a killer?" asked Jake.

"I don't believe that," said David flatly.

Jake quickly turned off the recorder. "We need to go to the police station and revise your earlier statement," he said. "In essence, you didn't precisely *lie.* They asked you when Rolly left and you told them.

Your other guest, Susan Dwyer corroborated that. They didn't ask you if Rolly returned.

"Additionally, *you did not discover the body together*. You, alone, discovered it, just as you stated. The fact is that you called Rolly in, *afterwards*. Of course, you were embarrassed about his presence, but you've decided that, at whatever cost to you, they need to have all the facts.

"Lying about sex is vastly more acceptable, David, than lying about the facts of a murder. Now, tell me again, did either of you touch anything before the police came?"

"No. I touched Marc to see if he was still alive," said David, tears filling his eyes, "even though I knew he wasn't. That's all. We went into the kitchen and talked, and then Rolly left and I called 911."

"Did Rolly have a car?" asked Jake.

"Yes. An old Toyota Corolla," said David. "I don't know what year. It's beige, I think."

"Could any of the neighbors have seen it?" asked Jake.

"I don't know. Maybe," said David.

Thoughtful, Jake turned his attention.

"All right, Julie, Joe. What have you got for me?" he asked.

"Marc was the owner of a private island, Castle Cay," said Julie. "He owned it in a trust fund, managed by his brother, Avram Solomon, in Boston."

She told him that, coincidentally, it was currently in the process of being sold.

"For *forty million*," added Joe.

"That is an interesting 'coincidence'," said Jake. "And who gets the money now?" he asked.

"Eventually, Marc's uncle," said Julie. "But the important thing - I think - is that David has *nothing* to do with the island or its sale! As for him inheriting this house, David was a joint owner, who put his *own* money into the property. The taxes and insurance are high here, too, and David has very little income. He was better off financially with Marc *alive*...particularly since the demand for Marc's work was taking off."

Joe leaned forward.

"We have some suspicion about the dealings of the brother, Avram Solomon, in Boston, Jake," he said. "I went to Castle Cay. It's an outer island in the Abacos chain, in the Bahamas, and it's obvious it was used for drug trafficking in the recent past...most likely while Avram Solomon was managing it, in the trust."

"But not now?"

"No. But, whenever it was, we think Marc Solomon knew nothing about it."

"He *absolutely* didn't!" said David.

"And, Jake, Marc was planning a visit to Castle Cay before signing on the dotted line," said Julie. "It seems that Avram Solomon, as trustee, now has the power to sign the deal."

"But he *doesn't* get the money," said Jake.

"No," said Julie.

"David, does your friend Rolly know Marc's brother, Avram?" asked Jake.

"I don't think so."

Julie felt compelled to speak up.

"Rolly is from Boston originally, though."

"Hm-m. Very interesting," said Jake. "Well…keep digging. You two are doing a good job. I'll be looking into this, too. Keep me informed, okay?"

They nodded.

"Well, David," he said, snapping his briefcase shut, "let's go get this over with, shall we?"

Julie and Joe went with them to the police station, where David revised his previous statement. An all points bulletin was issued for Rolly Archer, who was - by that time - nowhere to be found.

43

Rolly was as scared as a squirrel halfway across a turnpike. He was out on the Gulf of Mexico in a thirty-foot, fiberglass cabin cruiser named *Miranda* built in the early eighties. The wind was howling and driving the rain sideways, and the boat was dropping into twelve foot troughs. Rolly was an avid diver and a skilled sailor who had been caught in bad weather before, but he had never experienced *anything* like this.

He laughed at his own stupidity, as the boat lurched and slammed into the waves. How could he have expected David to keep his presence a secret? He'd had no choice but to run. There wouldn't be any bail or probation this time. He would go to prison!

Rolly figured that he would never get out of Florida in his car, that his only hope of freedom would be Mexico. But now, it looked like he might not make it across the Gulf. What a fool he'd been. What a stupid fool!

He wrestled with the wheel, struggling to stay on the southwestern course.

I shouldn't have taken the money!

I shouldn't have moved here!

No. That was bullshit.

No matter what, the Keys were the best part of his life. Rolly remembered how difficult it was growing up in Boston's North End.

His father had taken off when he was four, and he and his mother had ended up on welfare. She sank into a deep depression, from which she never recovered.

———

Rolly remembered her sitting there, mesmerized by the TV, in an apartment full of clutter. Paths wound through piles of junk from one darkened room to another.

Once in a while, she spoke to him.

He would have left, but there was no place to go.

His school life had been another kind of hell, controlled by a macho Italian gang. To fit in and survive, he'd learned to act as tough as the rest of them, but he lived in constant fear of being exposed.

When he finally graduated, he had immediately found a clerical job in a hospital and escaped to Brookline, far away from the North End.

The Art Institute was nearby and he registered for a course in oil painting. It had been necessary to change his schedule and work nights, and it took every extra dollar he had to pay for the twice-a-week classes.

That was where he met Marc Solomon, the rich and talented instructor's assistant and "star" student...who was openly gay. Rolly hated his guts.

⁓

The violent squall on the Gulf seemed to come out of nowhere, the sea suddenly rising up to an impossible height before him.

I only wanted to pay off the damn boat! Maybe I paid for my coffin, too...

44

J ulie and Joe parked the VW in Old Town next to a
cheery yellow and white house with gingerbread
trim. A sign read, *"Billie's Bed 'n Breakfast"*. David
had told them to park there, saying that Billie was a
friend of theirs, that she would recognize the car and
wouldn't mind.

They set off down Eaton Street, crossed Simonton
and turned left on Duval Street, heading for the
Sandpiper Gallery.

Old Town was bustling. It was a veritable mélange of
people, enjoying the warm, windy day…all colors, all ages,
gay and straight. Julie was reminded of Marc's paintings,
which were colorful and diverse like the city itself.

Shop doors were flung wide, offering everything
from brightly designed resort-wear to Conch Republic
items, like sponges and giant shells. Rainbow flags
whipped in the wind. Sidewalk cafes and bars hummed
with happy chatter, as some sipped coffee while others
clinked together their margaritas, toasting the day.

They passed Sloppy Joe's bar, still trading successfully on Hemingway's patronage since the 30's. Julie heard Jimmy Buffett music drifting from somewhere; she considered that it was Sunday, a weekend, and wondered if it was live.

When they reached the Sandpiper, the doors were open there, too, and Julie recognized several of Marc's paintings. Susan Dwyer was sitting at a small desk at the rear of the store and looked up as they entered.

She rose, smiling, and walked toward them, dressed in a billowy lilac and green caftan. She was a tall woman in her late forties, Julie guessed. She had broad shoulders and a square jaw softened by silver hoop earrings and shoulder-length, highlighted hair.

"Julie! It's good to see you!" she said, as they air-kissed. "Nice to see you, too!" she said, looking from Julie to Joe.

"This is my friend, Joe Garrett," said Julie. "Joe, this is Susan Dwyer."

"Nice to meet you, Susan," said Joe, shaking her hand.

"Did David call you back?" said Julie.

"Yes. I just got off the phone with him. I'm going over there later this afternoon. I have so much work to do! Marc's New York show is still scheduled for October 5th, you know."

"Yes," said Julie, "David told me."

"He would have wanted that," added Susan. "Can I show you around, Joe?"

"Please do."

Susan took her time, telling them a little about each of the artists whose work was on display.

Joe noticed some paintings signed *Roland Archer*. "Is that Rolly, Marc and David's friend?"

"Yes," said Susan. "He's an excellent artist. Not in the same league with Marc, though. Marc had a very rare talent. I'm expecting some of the pieces in the New York show to sell for several thousand dollars each."

A customer came in and Susan excused herself to tend to him. Seeing that she was going to be tied up for awhile, they waved goodbye to her and headed back toward Mallory Square.

When they reached Front Street, Joe said that he'd been to the seaport a few times and knew a good place for lunch. He was clearly headed for the pier, talking on about the food. Julie stopped, feeling light-headed and nauseous. Joe turned, and saw her rooted to the spot, ashen.

"Merlin? Are you all right?"

"Yes...but I'd rather not go out on the pier. Let's go back to the house."

"Okay, but can we sit for a minute?"

He took her hand and led her to a shaded bench. After she was seated, Joe remained standing, his foot on the bench.

"Julie...I know how your husband died," he began, "and I can understand your fear of the sea. I can't imagine how terrible that must have been.

"But one thing I know: fear feeds on itself and it grows like an invasive weed. It lies to you and closes in around you until you can't move.

"Right here in the Keys, there are delicate coral ridges more beautiful than you can imagine, Julie. They're protected and nourished by the very sea you fear so much…and they're teeming with life, not death.

"Someday, I hope you'll let me take you to see the other side of the coin…"

45

"There *is* a second buyer who is very interested in Castle Cay," said Frank Martino into his headset, using the stale ploy to nail down John Walsh, the lawyer representing Holiday Cruise Lines.

Attorney Walsh wasn't biting.

"Well, if Mr. Solomon can't wait for my client to consider every aspect of this contract in light of the new circumstances, perhaps he should sell to *them*."

Frank wondered what the hell he meant by that. Did they want out of the deal? Or were they angling for a lower purchase price? He was glad the man on the other end of the phone couldn't see the panic on his face. Fortunately, Frank had mastered a confident phone voice.

"Mr. Solomon is a man of his word, Mr. Walsh. He accepted Holiday's offer, and he will stand by his commitment to sell Castle Cay to your client for the agreed amount," said Frank. "And, of course, no one wants to see a buyer lose their deposit."

Take that, you wiseass. Now he was playing

hardball, and he had just whacked it into Walsh's court.

Addicted to winning, Frank felt a rush as the balance of power returned to his side. He rocked back in his desk chair, his hands locked behind his neck, swiveling around to see if any of his fellow agents had heard. Nick, in the cubicle across the aisle had, and Frank winked at him while he waited, silently, for Walsh to reply.

"My client just wants a thirty-day extension on the closing date, Mr. Martino. They have every intention of proceeding with the purchase."

Thirty days! I could be dead in thirty days.

Frank knew that he had no authority to negotiate. As an agent, he was required by law to present this request to his principal, Avram Solomon. Although that would be unpleasant, it wasn't the problem. The problem was a hundred grand Frank owed Joey Bonanno, his bookie.

Fuck. First the seller needs more time, now the buyer!

"Of course, I'll present your request to Mr. Solomon," he said in his best phone voice, his back now turned to his colleague across the aisle. "But, frankly, it could be the 'straw that breaks the camel's back', so to speak. Your client might be more successful asking for a two-week extension, Mr. Walsh."

Frank knew that was weak. The length of the silence on the other end confirmed it. The power had shifted. At last, the attorney spoke.

"Well, let's try thirty days first, Mr. Martino. Goodbye."

Fuck. Me.

46

The weather in Key West had deteriorated as the afternoon wore on. Julie looked out the glass doors and across the pool patio. The yachts on the far side of the canal were rocking, palm trees were swaying, and the intermittent rain seemed to be falling once again.

Joe was lounging beside her at the kitchen bar talking to David. Ostensibly, they were keeping him company while he prepared dinner. In reality, Julie knew that she and Joe were enjoying the new intimacy they'd found with each other. For her part, she was more relaxed now than she'd been in a long, long time. *I'm glad that he knows about Dan,* she mused.

Rolly's name caught her attention, and she tuned back into the conversation. Joe had commented on Rolly's paintings.

"Where do you think he would go?" asked Joe.

"I can't imagine!" said David. "He told me his mother died years ago and he has no other family."

"You better hope they catch him, David," said Julie.

"I hope they don't."

I give up, she thought.

The doorbell rang.

"That's Susan, I think," said David. "Would you get it, Julie? I've developed a phobia about answering the door."

Julie smiled and went to answer it.

"Hi!" said Susan, shaking off her umbrella. She snapped it shut and leaned it against the house. "It's raining sideways; I'm soaked. What a day to move paintings!"

"C'mon in," said Julie. "The rain seems to stop every once in a while. Maybe it will clear long enough to get them into your truck."

Susan had on a light blue denim outfit, the lower pant legs darkened from the rain. She kicked off her shoes and padded to the bar in her socks, exchanging hellos with Joe and David.

"Hm-m, whatever you're cooking smells great," she said, taking a seat.

"A pork roast, with red potatoes and asparagus. There's plenty; we were hoping you could join us?"

"Oh…I'd love to, thanks."

Julie noticed the hesitation and wondered if she'd had other plans. "I'm glad you can stay; I set a place for you," she said, picking up a bottle of wine. "We have Merlot, or there's some Chardonnay, if you prefer."

"Oh, thanks, but I don't drink. I'm diabetic," said Susan. "I'd love some iced tea, if you have it."

"Sure, I'll get it," said David, who had just finished slicing the roast. He brought her a glass and suggested that they go sit at the table.

"Why don't I go up and get the paintings first; it'll only take me a minute," said Susan, opening the portfolio at her feet and extracting a folded sheet. "I brought this to wrap them in, just in case the rain keeps up."

"Can I help?" said Julie.

"No need," said Susan heading up the stairs. "I only need a couple, and they're light before they're framed."

"You can help *me* Julie," said David. "I've decided to fill the plates in here. You want to go get them?"

"And what do *I* do?" asked Joe.

"You just sit there looking *manly,*" said David, with a wink.

Julie chuckled as Joe turned red…but he was smiling.

A few minutes later, they were enjoying a candlelight dinner and complimenting the chef.

"So, how are things coming with the show?" said David.

"I've already shipped most of the paintings to the Herzog Gallery, along with the details for the plaques," said Susan.

Looking at Julie and Joe, she explained, "You know…medium, date, and description." She turned back to David. "But enough about the show…how are *you* doing, David?"

"I'm numb, I guess. It's all too much. I just can't cry anymore. And now they're looking for poor Rolly."

"They're looking for *Rolly?*"

"Yes. I'm sorry, Susan. I lied to you. Rolly was here with me that night. We arranged for him to come back after he left with you."

Julie caught Joe's eye. He had picked up on Susan's body language, too. She wasn't surprised about Rolly staying over that night. No downward looks, no embarrassment.

"Oh," she said, pausing. "Do they think Rolly had something to do with it?"

"I don't know," said David. "But they're looking for him."

"Do you think Rolly could have killed Marc, Susan?" said Julie.

"Oh, no. Rolly? Of course not."

"Any thoughts about where he might have gone?" asked Joe.

"No idea," she said, shaking her head.

Susan had left, the dishes were cleared away, and they were relaxing in the living room. There was no more talk of Marc's death, or Rolly Archer. They kept the conversation light and watched the rain outside.

David turned on the local weather channel. The sharply dressed weatherman stood, gesturing, next to a computer-enhanced map.

"In the last forty-eight hours, we've upgraded this system to a tropical storm. You can see Carlo here, approaching Cuba.

"It's a large, slow moving system and a major rain-maker. So far, it's caused severe flooding in Haiti and Jamaica, and we're getting the outer bands of wind and rain here in the Keys.

"If the cold front in the south continues pressing down into Florida, it could disorganize this storm and push it back out into the Atlantic.

"However, if that front weakens, Carlo will likely head into the Gulf of Mexico, where the warmer water could cause the storm to strengthen and grow more organized. In that case, we would expect it to take a more westerly course, toward Mexico.

"Stay tuned to the Weather Channel here for continuous updates on tropical storm Carlo."

David turned off the TV. "Well, let's pray it blows out to sea," he said, sighing and getting up from the couch. "I hope you two will forgive me, but I'm so tired...I really must go to bed."

"Not at all, David," said Joe, rising. "Thank you for a terrific dinner."

"It was really good, David. Thank you," said Julie.

"My pleasure. I'm glad you're both here. Goodnight, my dears." He set his wine glass on the kitchen counter and went into his bedroom.

"He's such a nice guy," said Joe.

"Yes, he is," said Julie. "He's a gentle person. It's a shame he's embroiled in all of this."

An awkward silence ensued. Julie was reluctant to end the evening, but they had clearly run out of conversation. "Well, I guess it's that time for me, too," she said, rising.

"Yeah, good idea," said Joe.

She turned off the lights and headed down the hallway. His arm came up beside her, blocking her bedroom door. "Julie, wait," he said. "You're driving me crazy. I can't wait any longer." Then he pulled her into his arms and kissed her.

Julie succumbed instantly. She couldn't have said no if she wanted to…and she certainly didn't want to.

They undressed quickly, their hands all over each other, exploring secret parts they had longed to see and touch.

Joe yanked off the comforter and they fell on the bed. He paused, braced on his arms, looking down at her. Julie savored the delicious weight of his body on hers. And then he was moving inside her.

The rain pounded furiously at the window, but Julie was oblivious to it, caught up in a mounting storm of her own.

47

Rolly's stomach convulsed as the Miranda suddenly dropped ten feet after riding the crest of another mammoth swell. The rain had been coming in torrential hurricane-like bands. But for now, at least, the furious pelting had stopped. He estimated that the cloud cover was about eighty percent, but it was moving fast, the full moon showing through, illuminating the storm-tossed sea.

He couldn't calculate where he was. All he could do was try to stay on a west-southwesterly course. He thought that he might have been swept in a circle when the heavy rain came the last time. His struggle to keep the boat heading into the waves pulled him off course. It had been difficult to see. The squall was so violent the rain had blown around inside the cabin.

Soaked and exhausted, Rolly had unconsciously held his breath during much of that long, stress-filled battle. Now he began to breathe more deeply. His strength was depleted, and his body ached from head to toe.

Is this where it ends?
I just wanted a life.
A life that wasn't a lie…

———

Marc Solomon was filling in that day at the Art Institute in Boston, substituting for the art teacher. He circled the classroom, stopping at each easel to congratulate or critique each student's work.

"Your brush strokes are too tight. Too constricted," he said of Rolly's painting. "Don't be afraid to experiment! To let go! You're not a child and this isn't a coloring book. You don't have to stay within the lines. Do what you want to do, not what you think you have to do."

Rolly bristled. He thought that Solomon's comments were about more than painting and his embarrassment had swiftly grown to anger.

What did that conceited asshole know about anything? His painting was fine and his life was better than it had ever been!

Rolly had his own efficiency apartment. He'd been promoted at the hospital and he was earning enough to live on, even save.

And he had a special friend, too. His name was Ash, and he worked in the records department at the hospital. They'd met one day when Rolly was eating lunch in the cafeteria. The place had been jammed and, as usual, Rolly was sitting at a table by himself.

"Hi, do you mind if I sit here with you?"

The boy was so pretty that Rolly was dumbstruck. Ash had a slim body and he wasn't very tall. He had wavy brown hair that tended to fall over one long-lashed eye or the other, so that he had to reach up and tuck it behind his ear. His skin was a light coffee color...Indian, Rolly thought...and he had very white, straight teeth...a very beautiful mouth.

"No," said Rolly, finding his voice. "Go ahead."

They found it easy to talk to each other and began seeking each other out whenever they were in the cafeteria at the same time. Soon, they were coordinating their lunch breaks.

Rolly became obsessed with seeing Ash at the hospital. He fantasized about him at night. It seemed that Ash was interested in him, but he wasn't sure.

At last, they made a plan to meet for a movie. Rolly sat through it, staring at the screen, filled with desire. He yearned to touch Ash, ached for Ash to touch him. It was the most exquisite torture he had ever felt.

Rolly was in a secret limbo, loving it and hating it, all at once.

And then along came Marc Solomon, who criticized his painting...who criticized him and his life... in front of everyone.

Rolly stewed over it for weeks.

His attempt at free brushwork was a disaster. He overworked his colors and they all ended up looking like mud. The more he tried, the worse his painting became.

Was Solomon right?

Rolly made a decision.

One day as he and Ash were leaving the cafeteria in the basement of the hospital, he stopped at a door. "Come in here," he said to him. "I have to tell you something."

He never told Ash anything. He'd just locked the door behind them and kissed him on the mouth. There was no protest; Ash was as eager as he was.

In no time, Rolly's pants were down around his ankles and Ash was kneeling before him, blissfully changing Rolly's life...and inadvertently improving his art.

In the darkness of the Gulf, Rolly smiled, even as the rain began again.

48

J ulie woke up facing Joe, her head resting on his left shoulder and her left leg draped across him. She carefully extricated herself, trying not to wake him. Lying on her own side, she admired his long, lean body.

The light fuzz of hair on Joe's tanned skin was blonde from the sun, like the stubble of his beard. In his nakedness, though, Julie could see that his skin was actually much lighter… and his hair darker. He was beautiful.

How did I resist this man for so long?

Joe wore a rugged, stainless steel watch with a brown leather strap. Julie ran her finger lightly over a vein on his forearm, near the watch. He stirred, opened his eyes and then smiled, obviously remembering the night's activities.

"Morning, Merlin."

"Morning," said Julie, kissing around the left nipple on his chest.

"Make bigger circles," he said.

"Okay, but you can't move…"

⎯⎯

They joined David in the kitchen about an hour later.

"Good morning, you two. Did you sleep well?" he asked.

One look at them told the story. "Well…since you don't smoke…how about some coffee?"

It was still raining. David had turned on the TV to get an update on the storm. The weather picture hadn't changed much. Tropical storm Carlo was stalled over Cuba, causing widespread flooding. The gusting wind and rain in the Keys was predicted to continue and probably worsen. David was sick of listening to it. He picked up the remote control and changed the channel from the weather to the news.

"There is a new development in the Florida murder case of artist, Marcus Solomon. According to a source in the Key West police department, an APB went out yesterday for Roland Archer, another artist, and a friend of the victim. Roland Archer is now a 'person of interest'.

"We have learned that the police found Roland Archer's car in a grocery store parking lot. There is some speculation that the he may have left Florida in his boat, the 'Miranda,' which is reported to be missing from a Key West marina…"

"Oh, dear God!" said David. "Rolly's out there in the boat!"

As one, they all looked out through the rain to the huge white yacht anchored across the canal.

It was pulling its moorings taut...rising and falling as waves pounded the dock.

49

Rolly was slumped over in his seat clinging to the wheel, barely able to keep the Miranda's bow straight atop the swells. He was soaked to the bone, and the windshield was so wet and crusted with salt that he didn't know it had stopped raining. He was grateful for the meager daylight, though, and amazed that he was still alive to see it.

Somehow the Miranda had stopped fighting the waves and begun riding them. The compass said he was headed north. Rolly no longer cared. He was going to die. He would keep her straight as long as he could, but he was weak and he knew that the next whirlwind would take him under. Dark, threatening clouds stretched overhead. On the horizon, there was a faint, pink smear of sunshine…so far away.

He shivered.

No one could have foreseen all this mess. At least David would never know that Rolly took the money.

That was good. It would have hurt him so much, and he was already grieving.

David's sweet nature reminded him of Ash, and the long-ago love affair that had freed him in so many ways. Marc Solomon had noticed the creative part and suspected the rest.

"That's fabulous, I love it!" said Marc, looking over an oil Rolly was just completing. "The colors are so clear and vibrant. The impasto gives it great depth and power. Good job, Rolly!"

The whole class heard him, including the art teacher. Rolly was thrilled, and he stayed after the class to thank Marc.

"That meant a lot to me, what you said about my work. Thank you."

"Don't mention it. It's a terrific painting. You're very talented."

From that day on, Rolly had seen Marc as a role model rather than an enemy, and they had eventually become friends.

However, Rolly's childhood had produced a secretive adult. Despite Marc's urging, Rolly remained "in the closet". The liberating change came when Marc moved to the Keys and Rolly came to visit.

Key West was a revelation...gays were everywhere! They walked down the street holding hands! Rolly loved it

...the artsy, quirky waterfront atmosphere...everything.

After two more vacations, Marc convinced him to move down, to pursue his art in earnest. He even offered to show some of Rolly's work in the Sandpiper, an art gallery he and his agent had opened. And so, Rolly had moved to Key West.

He'd gotten a job at the Marina, cleaning, scraping, caulking and painting boats. He made creative signs and devoted his free time to his own painting. Rolly was a happy and fulfilled person for the first time in his life.

And he owed it all to Marc Solomon.

Of course, he'd met David, Marc's partner. He hung around with them, and enjoyed their company. He considered them to be a happy couple, which they were. Time passed, and their mutual friendship deepened.

One day in winter, the three of them were returning from a diving trip. When they got off the boat at the Marina, Rolly took them to see a boat he was working on, the 'Miranda'.

"What do think of her?"

"What do I think? I think she's a wreck," said Marc.

"Me, too," said David.

"No, she's actually seaworthy," said Rolly. "She just needs a lot of work. I've got three thousand dollars I could put down on her, and another thousand for parts and materials. But...I haven't got any credit history, and I can't get the other fifteen thousand."

"Eighteen thousand? That's pretty cheap for a boat this size," said Marc.

"Are you sure you can fix her up?"

"Positive."

Marc contemplated the situation.

"I'll loan it to you," he said. "We can fish and dive off her. She'll hold more gear than our boat."

"Are you sure?"

"Of course, I'm sure," said Marc. "After you got caught with my marijuana? I owe you, man."

Rolly was ecstatic. He bought the Miranda before the week was out, and by summer, she was in the water. He'd only made five payments when Marc came to his apartment.

"Rolly, I need to talk to you about David. He has a crush on you."

Rolly had known that, but he had hoped that Marc didn't. He was quick to reassure him. "You don't need to worry about me, Marc. I would never do that to you."

"That's just it, I want you to."

"To what?"

"To have an affair with David. More than that, Rolly. I hope it develops into much more than that."

Rolly was stunned.

"What! Why?"

"Because David and I don't have sex anymore. Because I have AIDS and he doesn't. Because he's a sensual person and he can't go on this way. Because I love him, damn it...and I'm dying!"

Tears streamed down his face.

It took Rolly a while to reply. He couldn't imagine such a calculated relationship with David.

"No, I can't do it."

"Look, he means everything to me, Rolly. Don't take this the wrong way but - if you do this for me - I'll cancel the debt on the Miranda. Please, just think about it."

A few days later, Rolly took the deal.

———

Weakly, Rolly clung to *Miranda's* wheel, trying in vain to minimize the old boat's sickening slide into a trough.

Your plan worked, Marc.

His head dropped at last, and everything went black.

50

There was no tactful way to broach the subject. Julie had flat out asked David about his Xanax prescription.

"Marc wouldn't have taken that because of his anti-HIV drugs. He was careful about his medications."

"What about oxycodone? Did Marc have a prescription for that?"

"Yes, he did, but he never wanted to take them; too many of his friends had become addicted to their pain meds. For the most part, Marc managed his pain with marijuana. When he did take a pain pill, he'd cut it in half...

"Oh, God, it's true, isn't it? Someone *murdered* him!" He began to cry and grabbed a handful of napkins off the kitchen bar. "But it *wasn't* Rolly!" he said. He turned - napkins pressed to his face - and hurried to his room.

Julie was sorry she had triggered his distress. *Damn. Now he's embarrassed; crying like that in front of Joe.*

"Poor guy," said Joe.

"Yeah…well, I could have handled that better," said Julie.

"No. You have a direct way of asking questions, Merlin. It's productive. And that's a professional opinion."

Joe's cell phone rang, and he flipped it open.

"Hi, Sherm!" he said, putting the phone on speaker, for Julie's benefit.

"Joe, listen…I can't give you details, but it's in your best interest, as well as the agency, for you to tell me everything you know about Avram Solomon."

"No problem," said Joe, eyes wide, looking at Julie. "Julie O'Hara is here with me. I've got you on speakerphone, is that okay?"

"Yes. Actually, that's good. Hi, Julie. In case Joe hasn't told you, I'm Sherman Dixon, and I'm with the FBI. Joe and I have been friends for a long time, so call me 'Sherm', okay?"

"Okay, Sherm," said Julie.

Joe began filling Sherman in on what he had learned since their initial conversation. He told him about his trip to Castle Cay with Will Sawyer, the evidence of drug traffic in the recent past, how the timing of it seemed to coincide with Avram Solomon's management, and the impending sale of the island.

"Slow down, Joe, I'm taking notes. Okay, go on."

Joe continued, telling him their suspicions in regard to Marc's murder.

"There are a couple of holes, though, Sherm," he said. "For one thing, Avram was in Boston when his half-brother, Marc, was killed here in Key West. We still think he could have pulled the strings, though. The guy that's on the run now, Rolly Archer...have you seen that on the news?"

"Yeah. What about him?"

"He's from Boston, too, Sherm," said Julie. "Avram Solomon denied knowing him to me, but Avram is a pathological liar, at the very least."

"The other problem is motive," said Joe. "We think Avram wanted to prevent Marc Solomon from going to Castle Cay; that he probably didn't want him to see the altered side of the island. Marc didn't know anything about that, so it might have caused a glitch in the sale. That looks like a pretty good motive...except that Avram doesn't profit from the sale! He's just the trustee. The money ends up with Matthew Castle, Marc and Avram's uncle," said Joe, looking at Julie, who was nodding.

"I've met Marc's uncle," said Julie. "Matt Castle is a good man, Sherm, and wealthy, I suspect. He's a respected attorney in Boston."

"Thing is, we can't figure out why the sale of this island is important to Avram Solomon at all," said Joe.

"Hm. Julie...I understand that you have friends who work for this guy...or used to. Can you give me their names, so I can contact them?"

"Oh." Julie paused, biting her lip. "I don't know if I can do that, Sherm. One of my friends works for him right now. That could put his job in jeopardy, and he has a family."

"Julie, I wish I could be more specific but, believe me, your friend is better off establishing some distance between himself and this man, Solomon. Cooperating with the FBI...now...is a good way to do that. If nothing comes of it, you have my word that any information he gives us will be kept confidential.

*"Can you call him...*now...*and tell him about me and this conversation? Can you do that?"*

"Yes, okay. I guess I could do that."

"Great. Thank you, Julie. Then call me right back. Joe? You still there? Do you have my cell number?"

Joe said he did, and they hung up.

Julie leaned forward, her head in her hands. "Oh, God, Joe; what have I gotten Pete and Joan into?"

51

Pete Soldano replaced the phone in its base. He had told Julie that he'd call her back, right after he talked it over with Joan. Now he sat in his living room, staring out a pair of arched windows that flanked the brick fireplace. His wife had gone out to their front yard to rake some leaves. It was chilly, and she had bundled up as if she were going out to shovel snow. He had teased her about it.

Pete could see her standing at the end of the driveway chatting with their neighbor, Anita. She was laughing…happy.

He knew he was about to ruin her day.

Joan nodded to the neighbor, turned and walked back into the house through the garage, into the kitchen.

"Pete? Have you seen the paper? I want to do the crossword."

"It's out here," he said.

Joan walked into the room, smiling. Her cheeks were rosy.

"You want to take a crack at it before I do?" she said.

"Not right now," said Pete. "Julie just called."

"Oh? Why didn't you call me?" she said, plopping down in the chair next to him.

"Joan. Julie wants us to do somethin'. I thought we ought to talk it over."

"So talk," she said, leaning back, her legs crossed and her foot wiggling.

"She wants us to speak with an FBI agent about Avram Solomon."

Both feet hit the floor and she stiffened.

"*What?*"

"Yeah, I know, I know. That's a little more than we bargained for," said Pete.

"I guess! You can't do that…you'll get fired!"

"Well, let me explain what else she said…"

"Forget it, Pete!" she said, standing up now and pacing. "I know you want to help Julie, and so do I…but you don't know that Avram had anything to do with Marc's death!"

"Sit down, and *listen* to me," said Pete. "This isn't just about Marc. Avram is *already* in trouble with the FBI, accordin' to Julie. And you know we've been thinkin' he's crooked for a long time! She said that the FBI guy is a friend. His name is Sherman Dixon. She says we can trust him."

Joan started to object again, but he put his hand on her arm. "Listen, Joannie," he said. "This agent said I should *'distance myself from Solomon'*. Think about it; if Avram's doing anything illegal with the dealerships…well, I'm a *General Manager,* for chrissakes! I don't want to be accused of anything! And Dixon promised to keep us out of it, if nothin' developed."

"Ohmigod," said Joan.

They sat there in their matching wing chairs, staring into the cold fireplace. Neither of them spoke, as they considered the possible fall-out from all this.

"I think we should do this," said Pete, at last.

"Yes. I guess we better…"

52

Sherman Dixon walked briskly through the terminal at Logan International Airport in Boston, glancing at his watch. It was Monday, September 24th, ten past two in the afternoon, which meant he was ten minutes late. His carry-on bag was slung over his shoulder. He would have preferred a bag with wheels, but he was too tall and he walked too fast. They never made the telescoping handles long enough or stable enough. The big, black man looked more like a professional athlete than an FBI agent as his long strides covered the distance between the gate and the baggage area.

He was wondering how in hell he was supposed to recognize special agent Robert Branson, who was picking him up. Branson had described himself as "an average-looking guy with brown hair, driving a gray Ford Taurus". But as it turned out, it didn't matter.

Shortly after Sherm walked through the glass doors and crossed the street, Branson pulled up in the Taurus. It seemed to be the only car, being passed and honked at by various car-rental shuttle buses. The window slid down.

"Are you Sherman Dixon?"

"Yes."

"Bob Branson. Hop in!"

"Welcome to Boston," he said after Sherm got in. "How was your flight?"

"Good. No problems," said Sherm. "Thanks for picking me up. Your timing was great."

"Not really. That was my fourth time circling around," he said, laughing.

"Got to keep the Homeland safe from airport bombers," said Sherm.

"Yeah," said Branson.

Neither of them laughed, too aware of the truth of Sherm's remark.

"I booked you a room at a Quality Inn close to our headquarters," said Branson. "You can check in anytime. You eat yet?"

"Yeah," said Sherm. "I got one of those bagged lunches."

"Good. I need to get you up to speed as fast as possible, Dixon. Plus, if you've got any info for me, I need it *yesterday*. You want to drop off your bag and go right to the office, or what?"

"Yeah. Let's get that out of the way, as long as it's close," said Sherm.

They left Sherm's carry-on in his room and headed for the field office. Branson wasted no time filling Sherm in.

"You know Silvio Tambini?"

"By reputation," said Sherm.

"He's the focus of the investigation," said Branson. "The Tambini family has been bringing drugs into the northeast, principally through Boston and Providence, for years. We suspected that they were coming in through the Caribbean, but they shut down before we got our ducks in a row.

"About ten months ago, an undercover agent in southern California made a connection in Mexico and was able to trace the stuff over the border, into California, Utah, and on into Massachusetts.

Then...nothing. We had all the players, all the exchanges. But where the hell did it end up? It's on the street here...that's for damn sure."

He stopped there, and pulled into a parking space behind a square, red brick, four-story building. He got out of the car and Sherm followed along, taking the elevator with him up to the fourth floor.

They entered a large, open room with a lot of desks and people, mostly men, many of them eating lunch. Branson signaled to a number of them to follow him as they passed. Finally, they were all assembled; eleven white men, one Hispanic and two black men, including Sherm...fourteen in all. They were in the conference room, seated around a big, nicked-up, rectangular table.

"This is special agent Sherman Dixon, from the Washington office," Branson began, introducing Sherm. The men around the table spontaneously said their names, acknowledging him, one by one. Branson continued with his intro.

"He's temporarily assigned to this task force. He has some inside connections in both Avram Solomon's company and his family…where there are some other things going on, I understand. So we're here to share information.

"I don't want anybody to hold back. Free questions and answers, all around. I've been giving him an overview; so let me finish up with that, first.

"As I was saying, Dixon," he said, turning to Sherman, "we traced the stuff coming into Massachusetts, and then it disappeared… a dead end. They're cutting it and storing it somewhere, but damned if we can find out where. But we know it's the Tambini family.

"Then this Avram Solomon's unlisted phone number turns up on Guido, 'Guy' Tambini's home phone log. There were calls to Solomon Chrysler before, but we never thought about it, because Silvio's son, Guy, drives a Chrysler. And this was no wrong number, either. It was a ten minute call. And Avram Solomon lives alone, so he was the one answering the phone, talking to Guy Tambini, who also lives alone, and who called Solomon's unlisted number.

"I mean, this was a surprise to us, Dixon. This Solomon looks like a damn pillar of the community! He moves around in society…he's at every charitable fundraiser…he's on the board of the museum! He's a successful businessman. His uncle is a prominent, respected attorney. He lives on Beacon Hill, for God's sake!

"So what's he doing talking to a Mafia boss? That was the question. So we started watching the Solomon dealerships and his townhouse. And everything looks as normal as apple pie. And then you started asking questions about him. And here you are…and I hope you can help us."

Branson sat down, and everybody looked at Sherm.

Sherman stood up and began to tell them about Joe Garrett and Julie O'Hara investigating the death of the artist, Marcus Solomon, in Key West, about Marc being Avram Solomon's half-brother. He also told them about the impending, multi-million dollar sale of the island, Castle Cay, which was evidently used by drug traffickers in the past.

"How does the death fit into our present investigation here, agent Dixon?" asked the gray haired fellow. Sherm thought his name was Jack, but he wasn't sure.

"I don't know," said Sherm. "But in the course of the murder investigation, they met with Avram Solomon's uncle…the attorney…plus a GM in one of his dealerships, and a former employee in his central payroll department.

"All of these people suspect Avram Solomon of criminal activity, and I've set up meetings with them for this afternoon and this evening to see if we can connect the dots. They are very concerned about confidentiality, but I'm sure I can bring agent Branson along."

"Is Solomon an official suspect in his brother's murder?" asked the Hispanic guy, who had introduced himself as 'Alvarez'.

"No," said Sherm. "He has a solid alibi. He was here when it happened. Another thing, he doesn't profit from the sale of the island. He doesn't appear to have a motive."

"Still," said agent Alvarez, "a murder and a multimillion-dollar deal happening at the same time?"

"Yes," said Sherm, "that's what has aroused all the suspicion surrounding Avram Solomon. He is both the brother of the murder victim and the trustee in charge of the sale, and there is some question as to whether Marc Solomon was cooperating."

"So who inherits?" asked the black agent at the end of the table. He was a studious looking man, probably in his late thirties, with rimless glasses. Not surprisingly, Sherm remembered his name, Thomas Bailey.

"I've been told the uncle, attorney Matthew Castle, at Connor, Castle & Mann here in Boston, inherits the bulk of the estate, agent Bailey," said Sherm.

"Maybe there's a conspiracy between Castle and Solomon," said Bailey.

"That's even weirder," said Branson, standing up. "The Castles are rich and they came over on the damn Mayflower. Let's stop speculating on the murder in Florida, and stick to the drug investigation here.

"Okay, Dixon. Your turn," he said. "What questions have you got for us?"

"I'm assuming you're working in teams," said Sherm. "Who's handling the surveillance of the Boston dealership?"

The gray haired guy that had opened the question and answer period raised his hand, as did the dark haired, mid-forties guy next to him.

"Sorry," said Sherm, "I didn't catch everyone's name on the first go-round. Is it Jack?"

"Yeah, Jack O'Brien. This is my partner, Mike Simmons," said the older man. "We've only been watching a few days. So far, we haven't seen anything unusual going on. We spoke with the local cops who patrol that area, and they didn't have anything much to say about Solomon Chrysler, either. They did mention that our guy comes back in after closing one night a week to work, but we haven't seen him do it. He waves to them when they drive by, they said. That's it."

"That could be interesting," said Sherm. "There's been some suspicion of money laundering. Solomon is more than the son of the owner; he's an accountant, and he's listed as both the President and Treasurer of the company. The Boston store is where all the money is handled; the other stores are satellite operations."

"Some suspicion? Got anything more solid than that? Anything we could go in on, Dixon?" asked Bob Branson.

"Not yet, but maybe today," said Sherm, thoughtfully. "The people we're meeting are highly credible, in my opinion, and they know this guy well. I'm beginning to think that he's the missing piece in *two* puzzles…"

53

Matthew Castle leaned back in his well-worn chair behind his desk at Connor, Castle & Mann, and regarded the two agents sitting across from him.

"I'm not at all surprised to have the FBI questioning me about my nephew, Avram," said Matt. "I'm only surprised that it took this long for it to happen."

"What, exactly, do you mean by that, Mr. Castle?" asked Sherman Dixon.

"I mean that I think he's a dangerous and unscrupulous man. I've known him since he was born. He was a horrible child. He beat his brother, Marc, so severely he had to be hospitalized when they were boys. My sister, Miriam, took him to a psychiatrist for a while. The change in Avram was astonishing. He never did *anything* wrong after that. At least, not while anyone was watching. He was solicitous, and overly polite to Miriam...it was sickening...I thought it bordered on mockery. But my sister drank it in like a thirsty plant."

"Were there any more incidents between the brothers?" asked Sherm.

"No," said Matt. "Marc was afraid of Avram. He stayed away from him."

"All the charitable work Avram Solomon does," said Bob Branson, "how do you explain that? It doesn't seem to square with your description of the man."

"It's an act, in my opinion," said Matt.

"Does your firm handle any legal business for Solomon Chrysler?" asked Bob. "Are they clients?"

"Not any more. Not since Milton Solomon retired," said Matt. "There was only the one dealership then, here in the city."

"So Avram Solomon is responsible for the expansion to two other locations," said Bob. "He must be a good businessman, at least."

"Oh, he's smart. No question about that," said Matt.

"Would you happen to know what law firm Mr. Solomon switched to, Mr. Castle?" asked Bob.

"I understand they're with Cardenas & Shaw," said Matt.

Bob Branson jotted that down.

"Are you personally aware of, or do you suspect, any illegal activity related to Avram Solomon or his business?" asked Bob.

"No," said Matt. "As I said, it wouldn't surprise me, but I don't know of any illegal activity involving Avram."

Sherman could tell that Bob Branson was essentially done with questioning Matthew Castle. He wasn't, however.

"The island, Castle Cay. It originally belonged to your family?" he asked.

"Yes," said Matt. "My father left it to Miriam, who was the oldest. She left it, in trust, to Marcus. Against my advice, she named Avram as trustee. I suggested my partner, Tom Connor, or myself. She thought that Avram was smart, and he would be 'a good conservator'."

"What do you know about the island?" asked Sherm.

"Nothing, really. I know a cruise line has made an offer to buy it. I haven't personally been there since I was a child. Frankly, I didn't like Milton Solomon very much. And, as I mentioned, I didn't like being around Avram at all. So, I had no desire to vacation there with them.

"Miriam generally came to visit me at home. She frequently brought Marc. My wife was fond of him and he got along well with my kids. Miriam would never bring Avram to my house, though. We never spoke of it, but she knew I didn't want him there."

Neither agent could think of anything else to ask Matt Castle that would be useful. Obviously, the man had strong negative feelings about Solomon, but that didn't help them any.

"Well, thank you for your time, Mr. Castle," said Sherm. "Please give us a call if you think of anything else." He gave him a card, and they all shook hands.

Sherman shook his head as they made their way back to Bob's car in the parking garage across the street.

"I hope we get more useful information from the Soldanos, Bob," said Sherm. "Sorry. I guess we wasted time with Matt Castle."

"No, we didn't," said Bob Branson. "We found out that Solomon has a mob lawyer…John Cardenas."

54

It was dark when the two agents arrived in Salem, Massachusetts…a city made famous by witchcraft and magic. Sherm was looking forward to meeting the Soldanos. Bob was hoping for a magical break in the investigation.

Pete Soldano answered the door.

"Hi. Sherman Dixon," said Sherm, showing Pete his identification. "This is Special Agent Robert Branson from the Boston field office."

Bob held out his identification, also.

"Hi," said Pete. "C'mon in."

Joan was nervously waiting in the living room. She stood as Pete introduced her to the agents.

"Nice to meet you," she said. "Please, sit down. Can I get you something to drink? You know, a Coke? Or some water?"

"Some water would be good, thanks," said Sherm.

"I'll be right back," she said, and left to get the water.

Pete Soldano couldn't help staring at Sherm Dixon. He'd had no idea that the man was black, or so tall. He'd actually had to duck as he came through the front door!

For his part, Sherm had pictured Pete and Joan Soldano correctly, except for their deep tans. He thought they looked like they lived year-round in Miami.

"I hope you don't mind that I brought another agent along, Pete. Bob has an interest in Avram Solomon, apart from Marcus Solomon's death," said Sherm.

"No," said Pete. "We made our decision to help…whatever you need to do."

Joan returned with four glasses of water on a tray, set the tray on the coffee table and sat next to Pete on the sofa.

"So, where do we start?" asked Pete, looking at the two men.

"I understand that you've worked for Solomon Chrysler for twenty years," said Sherm. "That's a long time. It tells me that you're a loyal employee, Pete. And yet, I know from Joe Garrett and Julie O'Hara that things have changed a lot over the years that have caused you to distrust Avram Solomon, or have some misgivings about him. Why don't you begin by telling us what has changed, what has bothered you?"

"Well, I guess I was just a lot happier working for Milton Solomon. Joan worked there, too, in those days," said Pete, looking at her and giving her hand a squeeze. "Milton had respect for people. And he didn't micromanage, you know? When he put someone in a position of authority, they were in charge of that department.

"At first, when Avram came to work there, he just handled the payroll department, where Joan worked. But after Milton's wife died, he gradually turned over more and more responsibility to Avram. Eventually, he called a meetin' and told us that he was retirin', and that Avram was the new President of the company. Of course, by then, we were expectin' it.

"I wasn't thrilled about it, but the good news was that the company was expandin' to Lynn, so I applied for the GM position. I got the job and that worked out good for us, because Joan had gotten into a fight with Avram over some payroll issues and really hated workin' for him. So, anyway, she was able to leave and be at home for the kids. That's when we moved here to Salem."

"What were the 'payroll issues' that upset you, Joan?" asked Sherm.

"Nothing important, you know, or illegal," said Joan. "Some paychecks bounced, and I thought there should be some reserve money in the payroll account, you know, so it wouldn't happen again? It was just a small thing. I suggested it to Avram and he was very nasty about it. He said that 'it was none of my business', you know, that I was just 'supposed to type the checks', or something to that effect. It was very embarrassing and unnecessary. I was glad we were moving here. It was an excuse to leave, you know?"

"So, is the payroll for all the stores done at the Boston location?" asked Bob.

"Yes," said Pete. "That and everything else. Except for individual car deals and financin', everything has to go through Boston and be approved by Avram."

"But, he must be a good businessman. Isn't there a third dealership now, in Waltham?" asked Bob.

"Yes. That's what really got me wonderin'," said Pete, shaking his head. "He's *not* a good businessman. He makes terrible decisions. Even after all this time, he still doesn't know his ass from his elbow about the damn car business!

"My store could be making a lot more money than it does, but I've got my hands tied. The Boston lot, and the store, too, is small. Too small to generate a lot of money...and it takes a lot of money to expand! So, how's he doin' it? Listen, Miriam Castle came from money...but not Milt. And, from what I heard, she didn't love Milt. I heard she left her money to Marc. So where is Avram gettin' the money to expand the business and live like he does? I just don't get it, you know?"

Sherm looked at Bob Branson. Bob was quiet... thinking. No one said anything for a minute or two.

"Why didn't they expand the Boston car lot?" asked Bob. "There's a defunct gas station next door. Why didn't Avram buy it?"

"Exactly! *They already own it!* See what I mean?" said Pete. "I would have done that, years ago. We've got more room than we need out in Waltham and not enough room in Boston. It doesn't make sense!"

The four talked a little more, Sherm and Bob thanked the Soldanos, and they took their leave, heading back to Boston.

"Sharp guy, that Pete," said Sherman.

"Yep," agreed Bob. "Solomon's moves may not make much sense for his car business, but they make plenty of sense for his drug business."

Sherman nodded.

Bob pulled out his cell phone and punched in a number.

"Jack? Are you and Mike watching Solomon Chrysler?"

"Good. Oh, yeah? He's there?"

Bob nodded and glanced at Sherm.

"I want you guys to circle the block. That way you can keep an eye on Solomon and see when he leaves. But, listen, I want you pay particular attention to the closed gas station on the corner. See if there's an entrance on the other street. See if anyone goes in or out of there.

"Don't slow down; don't stop. Just keep circling. Do it until midnight. Good. See you in the morning."

He flipped the phone shut.

55

What the hell are they doing now?

Avram saw the blue Camry coming up the street for the third time, slowly. At least, he thought it was them. It was dark out, and hard to see through the lowered mini-blinds on his office window.

Yesterday they mostly just sat there. Who the fuck are they? Not cops. Silvio's men? Feds?

He got up casually from his chair, papers in hand, and slipped out the partially opened door to the corridor. He saw the security guard across the hall in the glass-enclosed business office looking at a newspaper, and nodded to him, smiling. He went down the hall, opened the men's room door, and shut it without going in. He dashed into the service department and out a small door to the right rear of the building, propping it open with a bunched floor mat.

He darted across the narrow lot, ducking below the cars, to where he could see through the vinyl slats in the chain-link fence. The Camry was coming around.

Oh, fuck. Not now!

She was coming out of the gas station, locking the door behind her with her big, metallic purse over her shoulder. She hopped into the dark car waiting for her at the curb, and it pulled away. The blue Camry was right behind it.

Fuck. FUCK.

Avram quickly retraced his path back into the dealership, and slipped into the restroom. He flushed the toilet twice, then turned on the faucet in the sink. Shutting the door behind him, he went back to his office. The security guard was still reading the paper.

Avram sat at his desk, trying to think it through. Could they be Silvio's guys? Boston cops, undercover?

He grabbed the Mont Blanc pen and turned it obsessively in his hand, while he glanced out the window through the partially open mini-blinds. He couldn't see a damn thing; it was black beyond the window, nothing visible but headlights. He decided to leave, since he was done with his weekly task of adjusting the books.

He picked up his briefcase and left the office, switching off the lights and locking the door. He waved at the security guard.

"Good night, Ralph."

"Good night, Mr. Solomon."

Avram unlocked the Jaguar and tossed his briefcase onto the passenger seat. He was just about to get in when the blue Camry passed by…again.

They didn't follow the drugs! They couldn't have missed that pick-up.

He got into the car in time to see the Camry turn right at the red light, passing the old, darkened gas station again. He pulled up to the lights and watched the blue car slowly continue on. When the light turned green, he crossed the intersection and headed for his townhouse. He kept his eyes on his rear view mirror, but no one followed him.

They're feds. It's me they're watching. Time for Plan B...

56

Avram was organized. All the important records were at his townhouse in one place: the den. He sat in his desk chair and fed them into the cross-cut shredder, a few at a time. He'd planned carefully for this, for years. The Feds would try to charge him, *in absentia,* with money laundering.

Well, he wasn't going to make it easy for them.

Fortunately, Silvio Tambini had more places to wash his money these days, and he spread it around. Avram never really wanted to do it; he didn't need the heat. There was a limit on how much money could be run through a car operation, even a large one.

Avram had been careful. Solomon Chrysler's new car business was legitimate, and Avram had been downright meticulous about taxes, so there was never any undue interest from the IRS.

It had all been creative bookkeeping in the used car and service side. Essentially, Silvio Tambini gave Avram dirty money from the drug business. Avram, in turn, regularly sent large checks to dummy companies owned by the obscure friends and relatives of the Tambini family...payments for nonexistent cars, parts, paint jobs, storage, service contracts...whatever Avram could dream up and pump up.

Silvio got his own money back, cleaned, and Avram got a cut.

Over the years, it had added up. But the *real* money was the rent...rent for Castle Cay, and then for the warehouse in Waltham and the closed service station next to the Boston store.

Castle Cay, in particular, had been a gold mine for Avram. But now he hated the place! Even more than that, he had hated his brother, Marc, who had painted the far side of Castle Cay *just before* Avram took over managing it. Two paintings showed the east coast of the island behind the ridge *as it was*...before it had a seawall, an airstrip and two cement block buildings to accommodate drug smuggling.

The canvases were dramatic. Dark and different from his other ones, they drew attention...and Marc had painted the date on them.

That fag bastard...why did he have to date them!

Avram had become obsessed with acquiring the paintings ever since he saw them at Marc's art show in Boston.

He shook his head, as if to shake their image out of his mind.

They don't matter anymore. The game is over. I win, anyway.

Avram had a foolproof plan to simply disappear.

He thought about his bank. They'd find nothing incriminating there, because he'd never kept anything of real importance in the bank. He sneered.

I've got my own "lock-box"...

It was a new car, changed out yearly, sitting amongst a sea of other cars, on the Waltham storage lot. This special car's invoice and computer record would be *lost* for a whole year, until Avram *found* it at the year-end inventory audit. He would simply drive out there one night a year and replace it with a new model whose record would be lost for another year.

Avram was the only one with the keys to the car...this car with no record, which was *hidden in plain sight*...that had a black bag in the trunk with his new identity...a driver's license, passport and a sizeable amount of cash.

His plan was to act calmly, as if tomorrow was just another day. If he was right, they were watching his townhouse, too. He would go to the dealership, as usual, parking his Jag in the usual spot. He'd close the blinds in his office, *squinting* at the bright sun, just in case they were watching. Then he'd look up a new car in the back lot, the same model with dark tinted windows, and get the keys.

A couple minutes on the computer would transfer the vehicle identification number of the car he was taking to the Waltham storage lot. He'd slip on his rain jacket and cap, put the dealer plate in the back window and drive off. In no time, he'd be in Waltham, switching the cars. They'd never know he was gone...with luck, maybe not until the store closed. By then, he'd be on an international flight out of Manchester, New Hampshire.

He smiled at his own brilliance.

57

Robert Branson pulled into the portico of the Quality Inn at half-past nine on Tuesday morning, September 25th. Sherman Dixon was waiting outside on a wooden bench, reading the Boston Globe and drinking a cup of coffee.

"Morning, Dixon," he said, as Sherm got into the Taurus.

"Morning, Bob."

Sherman noticed that Bob had stopped to get coffee, too.

"I got a call from Jack O'Brien," said Bob. "They saw a woman go in and out of the garage next to Solomon's Boston store last night. She was carrying a large bag, and there was someone else driving the car. Smells like a drug pick-up. They didn't follow her, just kept circling like I told them. They left at midnight, reported no other activity. Solomon worked late, and went directly to his townhouse. The other team logged in his arrival there."

"Do they know who the woman was?"

"No. They said she had blond hair, wore high heels and was carrying big metallic bag over her shoulder. They didn't see her face," said Bob.

"I wonder if she's somebody in the Tambini family?"

"We don't know. But the guy driving the car was," said Bob. "They traced the plate. It was Vincent Santoro, Silvio Tambini's nephew."

"Is that enough to go in there?" asked Sherm.

"No," said Bob. "We need to watch the garage tonight, and follow the pick-up with another car. In the meantime, you and I are relieving the team in Waltham today. I want to take a closer look at that location. I pulled off the team watching the Lynn dealership."

"Yeah," said Sherm. "There's nothing going on there. Not with Pete Soldano in charge."

"No," said Bob. "You know, this Solomon is a real piece of work. It's amazing how he's stayed under the radar for so long."

They continued to speculate about whether Avram Solomon could be connected to the murder in Florida. Soon, they were pulling into the Solomon Chrysler dealership in Waltham.

"Appears Pete Soldano was right," said Bob. "There's not a lot of cars on this lot... they've got plenty of room."

"I bet the problem is that this is the only dealership on this road. In Lynn, there are several dealers in a row.

Customers like to hit more than one place at a time when they're shopping around for a car."

"Yeah. I do," said Bob.

They pulled into a spot in front of the showroom. A salesman separated himself from the pack out front, and sauntered up to them.

"Hi! Beautiful day! Al Giordano. Can I help you?"

"Yeah, maybe, I'm Bob Smith," said Bob, shaking the guy's hand. "I need something bigger for my business, but comfortable, you know? I was thinking about an Aspen. But it doesn't look like you've got much of a selection here, Al."

"Believe me, Bob, I can get you anything you want. What, specifically, are you looking for?"

"Well, here's the thing," said Bob, "I don't want to have to order it. I don't want to wait."

"No problem. Solomon Chrysler's been around a long time, Bob. It's a big outfit. Did you know we've got three dealerships? We've got a huge storage lot at the end of Warren Street, right here," said the salesman, indicating the street running along the side of the service department. "If we haven't got the vehicle you want here...*I guarantee you*...we've got it there."

"That's good to know, Al. Tell you what; I don't have a lot of time today. I stopped in for a quick look-see. Give me your card and I'll come back when I've got more time," said Bob.

The salesman's face changed in an instant. He knew a brush-off when he heard one.

"Sure," he said, handing Bob his card. "Have a good day."

The two agents got back in the Taurus and drove out of the lot through the Service exit, turning right on Warren Street.

"Ooh, that hurt," said Sherm, smiling.

"Hey, it's better to pull off a band-aid fast," said Bob.

Warren Street was mostly rural, spotted with warehouses. About a mile in, they came to the huge, unmarked storage lot on the left. The salesman hadn't lied. It was loaded with new cars. There was a padlocked chain-link fence around it, and just beyond the cars was a building that looked like a small pre-fabricated hangar.

The road dead-ended at the woods, where they did a u-turn. There was nobody around. Bob headed back toward the main road.

"Wait, Bob," said Sherm. "Pull in there, behind that warehouse, on the left."

"What for?" said Bob.

"The dirt road behind the hangar. It's not overgrown. Somebody's still using it," said Sherm. "Let's sit here awhile."

"Right. Good idea."

An hour later, a car came down the road and turned in at the hangar. Both men strained to see the license plate before the dark car disappeared behind the metal structure. About thirty minutes after it arrived, the same car left. Bob quickly scrambled out of the car and sneaked a look around the corner of the warehouse to confirm his hunch.

"It's Vinnie Santoro," he said, climbing back in the Taurus.

"Damn!" said Sherm. "Are you sure it's the same car?"

"Same car, same number. The lab has to be in the hangar!" said Bob.

"Right…with the old garage in the city for storing and distributing the stuff," said Sherm.

"Absolutely! We'll trace the pick-up tonight and hit both places tomorrow morning."

Both men were excited as they drove down Warren Street and hooked a left onto the main drag, heading back to Boston. They never noticed Avram Solomon pass them in a gray Sebring sedan, driving in the opposite direction.

58

It was noontime, and all the Task Force agents were gathered in the conference room of the Boston Field Office, except for Jack O'Brien and Mike Simmons, who still had Solomon Chrysler and the old, adjacent garage under surveillance. Agents O'Brien and Simmons had just reported in.

"So all's quiet, for now. No action at the corner garage and Solomon's Jaguar is still at the Dealership. The service department is busy, but, according to Jack, they're not getting much sales activity," said SAIC Bob Branson.

"Do we have the warrants yet?" asked Agent Bailey.

"We'll have them soon, Tom," said Bob. "I've already informed Judge Wallenski of the locations, the individuals involved, and what we expect to find. They're 24-hour arrest and search warrants. Thanks to everybody's hard work here, we've already established probable cause, but we can widen the net by tracing the pick-up to the drops tonight. The plan is to hit all five targets simultaneously, early tomorrow morning, before dawn.

"As you all know, this has been a long-term investigation involving the Drug Enforcement Administration, the Mass State Police, and the Bureau...a total of 200 law enforcement officers. For security reasons, I haven't notified the DEA and the State yet. But they're on 24-hour-alert, and ready to go."

Branson walked from the head of the rectangular conference table to a wall on the side, covered with charts, pictures, and information.

"Our main focus will be these five locations," he said, pointing them out. "Silvio Tambini's home in Newton. Guido Tambini's condo on the Charles River. Solomon Chrysler, Boston, and the adjacent garage, here. Solomon's townhouse on Beacon Hill, and the hangar at the Solomon storage lot in Waltham. We will split into our teams, join up with these other law enforcement agencies tomorrow morning, and serve the Federal warrants.

"Of course, there will be smaller fish picked up at the same time, all the way down the line. All right now; I want to go over your latest reports, cover any questions anybody has and get right to your specific assignments."

Sherman Dixon hoped he would be assigned to bring down Solomon.

Meanwhile, Guy Tambini was at his parent's house in Newton for a special lunch; it was Silvio's birthday. Several family members were gathered around a lace-covered table, laden with various Italian dishes. Silvio sat at one end of the table, and his wife, Annetta, at the other end. Silvio had just finished saying grace, thanking God for all their many blessings.

Guy's cell phone rang. He flipped it open. "Yeah? Fuck! I'll call you back."

"Guido!" said Annetta. "Watch your mouth!"

"That was Billy Bones," said Guy. "We gotta get out."

"FUCK!" said Silvio, slamming the table, shaking everything.

Annetta kept her mouth shut.

"Do it tonight," said Silvio. "Soon as it's dark."

59

It was mid-afternoon of the same day, and Matthew Castle was home early from work. He sat in his elegant Beacon Hill living room in his "compromise" chair. It was a recliner that his wife had grudgingly bought to satisfy his demand. In the end, neither of them was satisfied. Matt had wanted a big leather chair, not this narrow, fabric one. Still, it *was* a recliner. And because Sylvia hated it, it was definitely *his* chair, a personal oasis in a room full of antiques.

He had his nice, bright reading lamp, the Boston Globe, a fire in the fireplace and a beer. It should have been perfect…but it wasn't. He angrily dropped the paper on the floor and stared into the fire.

"I wish you wouldn't throw the paper on the carpet, Matt," said Sylvia, looking up from her book. "I hate to be a nag, dear, but the newsprint comes right off on things these days."

"Sorry," he said, picking up the paper and setting it on the coffee table. "I'm irritated, I guess. I can't enjoy it."

"Why not? What's bothering you?"

"That arrogant peacock, Avram," he said. *"Castle Cay is our island.* It's been in our family since the Civil War...*and he's practically giving it away!* He has never even called to ask if we approve of the proposed sale. For all we know, it may already be sold!"

Matt was usually a very calm and rational person, but now he was pacing back and forth. Sylvia couldn't recall the last time she saw him this agitated.

"It's not that I oppose the sale, necessarily, Sylvia. I just can't swallow the highhanded way he's dealing with it. Or maybe I should say *underhanded* way."

"Why don't you call him?" she suggested. "This has been bothering you ever since Marc's death. Why not confront him about it?"

Matt stopped pacing and looked at her.

"You're right. I'm going to call him right now."

He left the room, went into his study and sat behind the desk. He looked up Avram's home number. It rang several times, and then he got a generic "Please leave your name and number" message. He hung up angrily. Searching through the business card file, he found Solomon Chrysler, Boston, and called that number.

"Good afternoon, Solomon Chrysler. How may I direct your call?"

"Avram Solomon, please," said Matt.

"May I say who's calling, sir?"

"Yes. Matthew Castle."

"One moment, sir..."

Matt waited impatiently, listening to music interspersed with service department specials. At last, the receptionist came back on the line.

"I'm sorry, sir. Mr. Solomon isn't in," she said.

Matt was furious, certain that Avram *was* in, but ducking his call.

"Thank you," he said tersely, and hung up. *That's the last straw. I'm going down there and confront him right now. He's going to talk to me, damn it!*

"Sylvia? I'm going out; I'll be back in a while!" he called out as he put on his jacket and grabbed his car keys. He didn't wait for her response.

It was only a fifteen-minute drive from Beacon Hill to the Boston dealership. In Matt's frame of mind, it seemed even shorter. As he pulled into the car lot, he saw Avram's black Jaguar.

I knew that liar was here!

Matt walked into the showroom to the central reception desk in the back of the room. He deliberately calmed himself.

"I'd like to see Avram Solomon," he said.

"I believe he's gone out, sir," said the dark-haired young woman.

"Can you tell me why his car is parked out front, then?" said Matt.

"Excuse me, sir," she said, "but…are you Mr. Castle?"

"Yes, I am. I am also Mr. Solomon's uncle and it's important that I speak to him," said Matt.

"I'm sorry, Mr. Castle," she said. "We've looked everywhere for Mr. Solomon since you called. He's not here. I don't know why he left his car here. Have you tried him at home?"

"Yes, I have. He's not there," said Matt.

"I'm sorry. I don't know where Mr. Solomon is, sir," she said.

"Well...thank you," said Matt, with resignation. "Please tell him that I'm looking for him when he comes back."

"Yes, sir."

Matt left the showroom and got into his car. He sat there for minute or two, and then he pulled out his wallet, searching through it. He found the card, and punched the number into his cell phone.

"Dixon, here."

"Mr. Dixon, this is Matthew Castle. I thought perhaps I should give you a 'head's up'. My nephew, Avram Solomon, seems to be missing."

60

Sherman Dixon burst into SAIC Robert Branson's office. Bob Branson was on the phone with the DEA's Special Agent in Charge, Brian Torrington. Bob put his hand over the phone.

"What is it, Dixon?"

"Solomon skipped!"

"What?"

"He's missing."

Bob Branson took just a moment to process the news.

"Torrington," he said into the phone, "I'll call you right back. Something important has come up. I'll call you within ten minutes. Yeah, bye." He hung up the phone.

"Sit. Tell me," said Bob.

"I just got a call from Matthew Castle. He said Avram isn't at his townhouse or Solomon Chrysler, although his car is parked at the dealership in its usual spot. O'Brien and Simmons saw him go into the dealership this morning at nine-thirty," said Sherm. "They said he never came out, but nobody inside has seen him since this morning. Castle said they were looking for Avram all over the place, but couldn't find him. Everybody in the store thinks he went out. They have no idea where, or why he left the Jag out front. "

"Shit!" said Bob. "He knew we were watching the Jag! He took one of the other cars! He's had plenty of time to get on a flight out of Logan, or Rhode Island...even New York!"

Sherm nodded, rubbing a hand over his head. "We need to get an APB out on him right away, Bob."

"I'll get his name and description out. Have O'Brien and Simmons go in there, *now*," said Bob. "Tell them to find out who's in charge, and close up that dealership! Tell them to get the customers out, *tactfully*; but keep the employees there. See if they can figure out which car he took, what kind of a plate it had...the number.

"Shit! If Silvio Tambini finds out that Solomon took off, he'll clean house! The warrants are executable now. We need to move this timetable up."

"Damn right," said Sherm, "unless we want to raid empty buildings."

"I'll call the State police and the DEA. You get the teams together, Dixon. You and I are going back to Waltham."

Sherm was on his way out the door and already on his cell, calling Jack O'Brien.

61

It was dusk when Sherman Dixon drove down Warren Street in Waltham with a six-member FBI SWAT team, which, to his surprise, included Bob Branson. They turned quickly into the parking area of the warehouse on the right, opposite the car storage lot, and drove behind the large building where they'd hidden before.

The Massachusetts State Police had an eight-man Special Tactics and Operations team already in place on the other side of the hangar. The STOP team was split up; six hidden behind the stored cars, and two snipers in the woods.

The combined assault force wore dark, full ballistic armor. They carried sub-machine guns and assault rifles. Although Sherman was armed and wore a protective vest and helmet, he was not a SWAT member, so he would go in last.

Bob Branson had just alerted the STOP unit that an undercover DEA agent had confirmed that Vinnie

Santoro had picked up Guy Tambini. It was assumed they were headed for the lab here. The narc also said they met with four other men; two of whom got into the car with Santoro and Tambini, and two others who followed behind them in a truck.

And so, they waited.

It was fully dark when the car and truck turned onto Warren Street. They passed the hidden SWAT team and turned left on the dirt road behind the hangar.

The SWAT team waited four minutes and then scurried across the street and down to the hangar, hugging the side of the metal structure. Sherm was amazed at how quietly the team moved, despite being so heavily armed. Bob Branson was in the lead, with Sherman bringing up the rear. Bob held up his hand to signal the men behind him to stop.

The drug crew had backed the truck up to the door and left one man outside, armed with an AK-47. There was a low "*ph-h-t*" and the guard fell to his knees and then onto his face in the dirt as the police sniper's dart hit its mark.

Branson grabbed the guard's assault rifle, and the STOP team ran out from the other side of the hangar with the battering ram. The flimsy door caved in immediately, frame and all.

"FBI! FBI! POLICE! DROP YOUR WEAPONS! HANDS IN THE AIR! NOW!"

Everyone's adrenalin was sky-high. Sherman entered the building last. There were at least thirty people in the building, including the police. Most of the actual workers… cookers, cutters, and packagers…were minorities, and they all had their hands in the air. It was easy to spot the bosses. Sherm recognized Guy Tambini from the photo on the wall at the FBI field office.

Suddenly, guns were firing, the air was vibrating, and Sherm was knocked hard, back against the wall. He slid to the floor, trying to process what had just happened. A man next to him collapsed on the floor, blood shooting from his face or his neck. Then Bob Branson was in front of him, shooting. Then it stopped. Sherm felt like he was in a trance…like everything was in slow motion. He knew he was shot…but oddly, there was no pain.

"Dixon! You okay?"

Bob sounded far away. Then everything went dark.

62

On the same Tuesday, September 25th, at half-past six in the evening, the Miranda was in the northwestern part of the Gulf, out of fuel and tipping perilously as she crested one wave after another and slid into the troughs. She had been blown north of the storm, to a place where the rain had stopped. Rolly was slipping in and out of consciousness. He was strapped into his seat, being jerked around like a rider on a mechanical bull.

He didn't know it, but the Coast Guard was covering about 500 square miles searching for him with helicopters and boats.

A violent jerk momentarily aroused him, and he looked out the windshield.

The Eiffel Tower?

He passed out.

The oil company employees still left on the huge deep-water drilling rig were relieved that Carlo was headed west, well to the south of them, and no threat to the US coastline. They were located 270 miles southwest of New Orleans, and during the day half of the crew had elected to leave. But now, to the west, beneath the clouds, the remaining crew could see pink and purple streaks from the setting sun, and the rain had stopped.

The environment on the 200-foot tall derrick and its platform was hazardous, the threat of an explosion ever present. It required the men's full attention at all times. The smell of oil and grease permeated everything, and they wore earplugs to protect themselves from the deafening noise as they went about their work. Given that, it was somewhat surprising that anyone noticed the *Miranda* at all.

Ken Pritchard was an engineer. He'd been working his tail off all day. He had just stretched, straightened up his back and taken off his hard-hat for a minute. He twisted his neck around to relieve the ache.

"Hey! There's a boat out there!" he yelled, signaling to the man next to him.

They began waving their arms, pointing.

"*She's going to hit the rig!*"

There was absolutely nothing the men could do to stop it. The boat was too close, and the huge swells were pushing it too fast. Nothing like this had ever happened before in all Ken Pritchard's years working for the oil company.

He braced himself, watching helplessly, wondering if the guy in the boat was dead, and wondering if they'd be next. He was thinking what every other man on the rig was thinking:

Would the collision tear the rig from the well a mile down?

63

Tuesday, September 25th, was a long day for Julie and Joe in Key West. The pleasures of the night couldn't dispel the daytime gloom at Twelve Gulf Wind Drive. David was inconsolable. The probability of losing Rolly after losing Marc was a one-two punch to his heart. The sun was setting and David had begun crying, once again retreating to his bedroom.

At last report, Tropical storm Carlo was making landfall on the Yucatan Peninsula. Florida had been spared, but dark clouds moved over the Keys and continued to whip up the warm waters of the Gulf.

Julie and Joe stood at the window, watching the yacht across the canal in fascination.

"Good God!" said Julie, shivering as she watched the violent water tossing the big yacht like a toy. "It looks like it might break loose!"

"I don't think it will break the lines, but it's going to be banged up pretty bad before this is over, even with all the tires along the dock," said Joe. "I'll tell you one thing, Merlin. If Rolly Archer is out there in a small boat, he isn't coming back."

"I've been thinking about that. I think Susan knows more than she's saying about Rolly," said Julie. "The Sandpiper was closed today; I called earlier and got voicemail. She's probably at home working on the paintings. I think I'll go over there, Joe…talk to her a little more…see what else I can find out."

She grabbed the keys to the VW off the bar.

"Want me to come with you?"

"No…please stay with David," she said. "He'll be out again soon, and he needs company. I won't be long."

64

Susan Dwyer hung up the phone, wondering where the hell Avram was. She had tried to reach him on both his home number and his cell phone. She thought that he must be working late, and it irritated her because she was forbidden to call him there. She wondered if he'd heard about Rolly Archer taking off. What a stroke of luck that was! After all, who would run, if they weren't guilty?

She studied the two dark paintings she was about to put in the crate. She couldn't wait to tell him that she had his precious paintings! She couldn't, for the life of her, imagine what he saw in them. As far as she was concerned, they were *depressing*. He should have just asked Marc for them, anyway, even if they weren't for sale. They were brothers, after all! But no, it fell to her to lie to Marc, telling him there was an "anonymous" buyer who had offered fifty thousand for the pair.

And then, unbelievably, Marc had turned it down! Who did he think he was, Picasso? Marc had gotten pissed with her for showing them at all. How was she supposed to know he didn't want anyone to see them? That they were *private*? How stupid was that? Did he paint to sell, or what?

He wouldn't let her take them to New York. And David wouldn't, either. *Oh, well, that problem is solved,* she thought. *By the time David discovers they're missing, they'll be sold to that anonymous buyer.*

She smiled and slid them, one at a time, into the crate, which was already addressed to Avram at his townhouse in Boston.

Meeting Avram Solomon was the best thing that ever happened to Susan; and it had happened at just the right time. Her carefully balanced world was about to fall apart like a toppling stack of blocks.

It had all started with her beautiful home. The two-story, waterfront house in Old Town, near Southernmost Point, was over one hundred years old. Two years ago, she'd put her life savings into the historic home. The real estate bubble was fully inflated at the time, and investors were buying property in the Keys like the sand was twenty-four-karat gold dust.

Susan had known the owner of the house, an old widow who was a regular visitor at the Sandpiper. When the widow told Susan that she wanted to sell the dilapidated house and move to St. Augustine to be near her daughter, Susan had immediately made the widow an offer.

Susan's plan had been to fix it up, and flip it. The mortgage payment was high, but doable, and there was no doubt in her mind that the house would sell quickly.

Unfortunately, everything had gone wrong. The repairs were *much* more expensive than Susan had thought. Just repairing the long dock had cost ten thousand! Susan didn't have enough furniture, and decorating was more costly than she'd planned, too. Then the real estate bubble burst, and suddenly there were a slew of houses for sale in Key West…and no buyers.

Meanwhile, the monthly payment on her adjustable rate mortgage had doubled, as had her property taxes and insurance.

Susan had been barely managing the situation by using up the available credit on her cards. The only bright spot was the increasing prices and demand for Marc Solomon's paintings. Fortunately, Marc had been prolific, and there was a backlog of his work at the gallery that had been selling well.

But that stockpile of his art wouldn't last forever, and, due to his illness, Marc had been slowing down. To make matters worse, they hadn't been getting along. The run-up to Marc's Boston show was a disaster. They couldn't agree on which pieces to show, or pricing, or much of anything. He drove her crazy.

Susan wanted to kill him!

And then she met Avram Solomon.

Susan first noticed Mr. Tall, Dark and Handsome studying the Castle Cay paintings. He seemed so intent...

"Hi," she said. "They're very dramatic, aren't they? Do you like them?"

"Oh. Ah...yes. Yes I do."

"I'm afraid those two aren't for sale. But, perhaps I could help you select something else. I'm Susan Dwyer, Marc Solomon's agent."

He smiled at her and grasped her extended hand in both of his.

"It's a distinct pleasure to meet you, Susan," he said, looking into her eyes. "I'm Marc's brother, Avram Solomon."

"My goodness!" she said. "I can't believe we haven't met before this!"

Avram turned on his considerable charm, and Susan basked in his attention. They walked around the gallery together for at least a half hour, until she realized that she was neglecting her job. She knew that Marc didn't like his brother, and she noticed him looking at her as if to say, "What are you doing with HIM?"

"I better get back to circulating, Avram."

"How about after the show? I know a great place for a late bite."

"Ooh, I don't know," she whispered. "I should probably eat with Marc."

"C'mon, there's a piano bar...it'll be fun," he whispered back. "Make an excuse! Marc doesn't have to know."

Susan was forty-six and lonely.

They slept together that same night in her hotel room, although 'slept' certainly didn't describe it. Susan was a big-boned, plain woman, who translated Avram's voracious sexual appetite as 'desire'. He used her and abused her...and she loved every minute of it.

Susan never felt so desirable in her life.

He'd flown her up to Boston twice after that, to spend the weekend with him at his townhouse. He overwhelmed her with his wealth, showered her with attention.

They were out to dinner at an exclusive restaurant when he began to talk about Marc having AIDS, about how he would certainly die soon, and what a terribly painful end that would be for him. Then he moved on to how devastating Marc's illness would be for her and the gallery, too.

"And, Susan, you know how much I care for you...I think I might be falling in love with you...and because of that, I did some investigating. I hope you don't mind that I did. It's the way things are done in my circle, when one is serious and contemplating marriage."

Susan had caught her breath.

"Oh, no! I understand, Avram!"

"Good, I'm glad. Now...I know that you have some liquidity problems because of the current real estate market. Heaven knows how many people have gotten caught in this downturn! Anyway, it seems that you have a problem, and so do I.

"You see, I can't bear for my brother to have a long and painful death; I would prefer that he pass painlessly in his sleep. And I was thinking, my dear, that if you were to help me with this, perhaps I could help you by buying your home. In the long run, it would be a good investment. And, who knows? We may be married one day, anyway."

The turn Avram's proposal had taken and the audacity of it, stunned Susan. And it showed in her face.

"I hope I haven't upset you!" he said, taking her hand, looking earnestly into her eyes. *"I would never want to do that, my dear! It's just that...well, I'm a practical man...and this seemed like a better way for all concerned...don't you agree?"*

Susan said nothing. She was speechless.

"Well, I'll give you time to consider my proposal," said Avram, skillfully and deliberately using the word 'proposal' once again.

"Let me know when you get home. I'd like to make some plans for our future! But whatever you decide, dear, I hope you'll save those two paintings for me when Marc does pass away. I presume you'd have them then, wouldn't you? I'd still be willing to pay fifty thousand for the pair."

At last, she found her voice.

"I...I'll think about it, Avram."

Susan could think of nothing else as she flew home to Key West. Avram had certainly done his homework. To make such a daring proposal, he had to know all *about her. Part of her was wounded...but part of her found it exciting. Avram took what he wanted! Susan felt a thrill, connecting his ruthless proposal to his rough command in bed. And then she weighed her situation with Marc against her relationship with Avram.*

She shouldn't kid herself about Marc. He didn't know the first thing about promoting himself or his work. Without her, he'd be nowhere. But Marc felt no loyalty toward her, and now that he was becoming "known", what was to prevent him from dumping her?

Nothing.

And if Marc were gone...a suicide, say...the value of his work would double, perhaps triple. She owned a number of pieces, herself. And she would probably retain the contract to sell the others. And she would get the gallery, too. And Avram could buy the house.

Susan had come to the conclusion that Avram was right...

It was "better for all concerned".

Susan shoved the crated paintings into her large walk-in pantry to get them out of the way, and closed the door. She began picking up all the loose Styrofoam on the trestle table in her kitchen, where she often worked. She was about to frame the other oil she'd taken from Marc's studio that was actually going to the Herzog Gallery in New York.

It was a small jewel of a painting; a sailboat against a vibrant sunset, the pure white spinnaker dead center.

Dead.

She really had to stop thinking about it! What was the point? It wasn't like she could change anything now. But, try as she might, she couldn't stop remembering. If only Marc *had* been dead…

David invited Susan over for a dinner of braised short ribs, after she teased him about how she had missed his cooking. She acted surprised and pleased at the subsequent invitation and offered to bring the wine. David, always an eager host, said he'd invite Rolly, too, and the four of them would "make a night of it".

She arrived at their house on Gulf Wind Drive about seven.

"I hope you boys like this Cabernet," she said, handing it to Marc. "It's called 'Chateau Very Expensive'! I poured two bottles into this decanter because the guy at the liquor store said it should 'breathe'."

They all laughed.

She was so nervous, but it was really easy. Since she never drank because of her diabetes, nobody expected her to drink the wine. David commented at one point that it had "an interesting finish", but no one else said anything about the taste.

Susan could tell as the night wore on that the alprazolam was working. All three of them were yawning...so she pretended to yawn, too.

"Well, it's time for me to go home, boys," she said, rising and retrieving the empty Waterford decanter. "Thank you so much for a wonderful dinner, David."

"I should go, too," said Rolly, yawning again. "I have to be at work early tomorrow."

Susan hoped Rolly wouldn't fall asleep at the wheel and have an accident. Marc and David walked them to the door, and they all air-kissed and said goodbye.

She returned an hour later and parked her car down the street. The lights were out, but to her surprise, Rolly's old Toyota was back in the driveway. She almost ran back to her car! But then she realized that there was no chance he'd be with Marc. He'd be on the other end of the house, just as drugged as David.

She ducked down below the level of the windows and circled around to the rear of the house.

She was dismayed to see that the light in the pool was lighting the whole damn patio. And Marc's vertical blinds on the sliding glass doors weren't closed all the way, either...

To hell with it, she thought. If I get caught I'll say I needed to get an extra painting to replace one I sold at the gallery. I'll say I forgot to ask Marc for it after dinner, and I didn't want to wake anybody. It was HIS idea to give me a key.

Susan quickly crossed the patio and paused on the outside stairs to the loft. There was no activity that she could see in Marc's room through the blinds. She climbed the stairs to the little deck and started to unlock the studio door, fumbling with the key. The latex gloves made it difficult to hold on to; she was afraid of dropping it.

Finally, she got the key in and the door opened. She closed it behind her, crossed the room and headed for the stairs that led down into the kitchen. She paused on every other step, listening for any sounds in the house. There were none; it was quiet. The luminous pool outside cast a dim light through the glass doors into the house, and as her eyes adjusted, she found that she could see quite well. She turned left at the bottom of the staircase and went straight down the short hall to Marc's bedroom. She put her ear to the bedroom door and listened for a minute or two.

Snoring.

Damn. He wasn't dead.

Susan had hoped that the combination of Marc's multiple HIV drugs and an overload of alprazolam would be lethal. However, she had always known that there was a chance it might not be enough.

No matter. If it wasn't enough to kill him, she knew the overdose would certainly knock him out. Unfortunately - and besides being ineffectual - that could create another problem. What if Marc slipped into a coma? She certainly couldn't have that! So, if need be, she had come prepared to quickly finish the job and leave.

She removed the syringe from the small purse strapped to her waist, turned the levered handle down and pushed open the door. The squeaking hinge sounded like a burglar alarm and she froze, holding her breath, halfway into the room.

No movement. He was still snoring.

She exhaled with relief, taking in the scene. Marc was sprawled on his back, naked and slick with sweat, despite the coolness of the room. Moonlight sliced through the partially open verticals, casting a striped pattern of light across his body. The ceiling fan made a low, hypnotic sound and was spinning so fast its blades were invisible. The weighted bottoms of the vertical cloth slats moved silently in the breeze. Within reach on the nightstand, a plethora of prescription drugs stood ready to aid sleep or relieve pain.

Surprisingly, the needle slipped right into the vein on the first try.

If there's a hell, I'm going there.

Marc's eyes fluttered open.
"Susan?"
Then they closed.

65

"Susan?"

Julie knocked again on the windowed kitchen door. She could see Susan standing by an oak table which held a small painting on an easel. She seemed to be staring into space.

"Susan?" she said, a little louder.

Susan turned and saw her. She was surprised, as Julie had assumed she would be, but she smiled and opened the door.

"Well, hello!" she said. "Come on in."

"I hope I'm not interrupting your work, Susan," Julie said, apologetically. "I just felt like getting out of the house after all that rain, so I went out for a drive. Marc told me so much about this old house and the way you restored it. By the way, it's beautiful! Anyway, I was driving by to see it, and I thought I might as well drop in and say hello. But, if you're busy… that's okay…I can let you get back to your work."

"No, no. That's fine...I'm glad you stopped by. I was just getting ready to frame one of the paintings I picked up the other night. I'm trying to decide on a frame. What do you think? Gold? Black? Wood? I'm thinking gold."

"Oh, I love this painting," said Julie, looking at the canvas on the table. "Definitely gold."

Susan held the little painting up. "There's so much gold in the sunset here...it has to be a little darker than the deepest gold tone. Antiqued, I think."

"Yes. I think that would be perfect."

"So," said Susan, returning the painting to the easel, "would you like some coffee, or tea?"

"I'd love some tea. I've had so much coffee lately."

Susan filled the teakettle with water and turned the gas on under it. "Do you mind if I finish framing that while we visit, Julie? It's the last one I have to do, and I'd like to get it out of the kitchen."

"Please...go right ahead."

"Okay. This is a small size canvas," said Susan. "I've got a frame in the den that I think will work, if I have all the pieces. I'll be right back. The tea and the cups are in the cabinet next to the sink, if you want to get them."

"Sure."

Julie went to the cabinet and took out two cups and a box of Earl Grey tea.

Only one teabag...

She opened two cabinet doors, looking for another box of tea.

Dishes, glasses...

She opened a door...a pantry.

There it is, past the coffee...

There was a tall narrow crate in the middle. She slid it to the side, exposing a name...

AVRAM SOLOMON

Julie sucked in her breath. The top of the box wasn't sealed up. It was filled with loose Styrofoam. She quickly brushed some aside exposing the top of a canvas. There were three letters on top: SFN

Suddenly she realized she was reading the letters on the canvas frame backwards. It was NFS...Not For Sale. And there were two. *Marc's Castle Cay paintings that he said he'd never sell.*

Julie's eyes drifted upward to a large Waterford decanter that sat on the shelf behind the crate. With a sickening feeling, she recalled what David had said about the dinner party the night of Marc's death:

"I usually get up during the night, but we finished off a whole decanter of wine and I slept right through..."

66

"Want some dinner, Joe?"

"Sure, I'm starved."

David began to pull out pots and pans, happy to escape any conversation related to his earlier, tearful retreat.

"Hey, David, did you get the photos of Castle Cay in your email from my friend, Will Sawyer? Julie said to send them here."

"You know…I haven't checked my email for days. It's probably *miles* long. Let's go see."

Joe followed him into his bedroom, and David sat at his desk.

The computer finally booted up.

"Was I right, or was I *right?*"

"You were right," said Joe, laughing.

David scrolled through until he came to *sawyerphotos.com.* He opened it up, and there were all the photographs.

"Oh, it's *gorgeous*," said David. "I didn't realize how beautiful it is. All I've ever seen are those two dismal paintings upstairs."

"See the wall and the airstrip here, David, those little block buildings? That's what we were talking about."

"Is this the Atlantic side? Where's the area that's in Marc's painting?"

"That's it, I think," said Joe.

"It can't be. There's a little point of land sticking out with water shooting up. It's right in the middle of the painting, with moonlight shining on it. Sort of the focal point, you know?" said David. "Marc told me it was where Julie's husband died.

"I'll be right back; I'm going up and get that one."

Joe was about to say that drug traffickers doing that much building wouldn't have much of a problem straightening out the island's edge to accommodate a sea wall...but David had already sprinted upstairs to the studio.

Joe was opening a message from *jsoldano* when David returned.

"They're not there! I can't believe she took them!"

"Who? Susan?"

"Yes! Marc specifically told her *not* to show them, that they weren't for sale!"

"Wait a minute, please, David..."

The email Joe was reading was sent on the 21st of September:

Julie,

I found a brochure from Marc's show and it had a picture of his agent. She's the woman we saw with Avram. I remembered her because I was trying to look at the Castle Cay paintings and they were blocking my view.

We feel like dopes! I don't know what made us think she was his date!

LOL,

Joan

Joe knew; it was their body language.

67

"You have caused me *such* a problem, Julie," said Susan, standing at the pantry door with a gun in her hand. "Come out of there! Sit at the table, while I figure out what the hell I'm going to do with you!"

"Susan. I'm sorry. I didn't mean to pry. I was just looking for tea bags."

"It doesn't matter now, Julie."

"It doesn't *mean* anything," said Julie, desperately, "just because you're sending paintings to Avram doesn't mean…"

"Oh, SHUT UP!"

Susan was pacing back and forth.

"What about Rolly?" asked Julie.

"What about him? The dumbass is probably out there, drowned, eaten by sharks! Who gives a shit?"

Susan, frowning, stroked her chin with her left hand.

She's worried; I'm a monkey wrench.

Susan raised her eyebrows and lifted her chin slightly.

Uh-oh. She feels back in control.

"Get up. We're going out for some fresh air."

Julie got up and Susan got behind her, poking her in the back with the gun.

"MOVE IT! Through there!"

She pushed Julie through the darkened house, through a dining room and a living room walled with big windows looking out on the sea…to a glass paned door.

"Open it!"

Julie opened it, stumbling forward on the threshold. She fell on her hands.

"Get up!" said Susan, whacking her in the back with the gun.

The pain tore through Julie as she staggered to her feet. They were on a wide wooden deck with a few stairs leading down and a long…very long…dock.

"Go on, hurry up!" said Susan, poking her toward the stairs.

"What are you doing?" said Julie, unable to keep the panic out of her voice.

"Shut up and walk! FASTER! I haven't got all night! I still have to get rid of your stupid car, you bitch!"

Susan angrily pushed her again.

It was dark and the tide was high, rough from the storm. The angry black water stretched ominously before her.

Julie ran like hell and jumped in.

68

"Yes! RIGHT NOW! Her life is in danger!" Joe yelled into the phone.

As soon as he realized it was Susan Dwyer who was connected to Avram, he had immediately called the Key West police. He told them to call Chief Sanders at home and then hung up.

Joe was scared to death that it was already too late.

It had all come together for him, as he sat at David's computer. It was about drugs. *Avram Solomon was still involved in the trade, even though they weren't currently using Castle Cay.* The construction there was damning. As long as the island was under his aegis, it implicated him. He wanted to get rid of it, especially to a company that would erase all traces of drug trafficking.

Joe and Julie had given Avram too much credit for rational thinking.

Marc had dated the paintings of the island and created a time frame for the illegal activity. Avram wanted them, just like he wanted Marc out of the way. It was about obsession and pathological control.

Joe didn't know how Susan Dwyer had gotten involved in all of this. But one thing was certain:

Susan wasn't rational, either.

69

The crack of the gun was the last thing Julie heard as she sank in the sea. It was opaque, full of sediment, and maybe twenty feet deep. She had jumped straight down, and now she stayed on the bottom under the dock, holding her breath in water that was moving violently and as numbing as a full-body ice pack.

Julie clung to the thick, slimy piling, thanking God for the barnacles that gave her something to grip. All the same, she tried not to cut herself, scared stiff to *bleed* in that roiled, muddy water. It was terrifying not to be able to see beyond arm's length! But she quickly realized the murkiness was a *good* thing because it meant that Susan couldn't see her, and *Susan* was far more dangerous than anything in the water.

Julie's lungs were exploding; she had to have some air! Slowly, she let herself rise to the surface.

"...ARE YOU, BITCH? YOU CAN'T STAY DOWN..."

Quickly, Julie sucked in the deepest breath she could manage and pulled herself down again beneath the dark, frigid water. Susan's garbled voice instantly faded away.

Clinging again to the thick piling, Julie hung on for dear life against the powerful, swirling current that threatened to tear her away. She waited and waited until she couldn't hold her breath a moment longer and was forced to come up for air.

Hand over hand, she rose to the surface, garbled sound becoming more distinct. There was tramping and yelling, men's voices. She broke the surface of the water out of sight under the dock, gratefully gulping a lungful of the salty air.

"...DOWN! PUT THE GUN DOWN! DO IT NOW! NO! DON'T...!"

Gunfire cracked again and there was a thump on the dock right over Julie's head.

"OH, SHIT!"
"IS SHE DEAD?"

She? It was Susan. Susan was shot! Julie moved to the outside of the piling, straining to see.

"HERE! I'M HERE! HELP ME!"

Suddenly, Joe appeared above her.

"MERLIN! HANG ON! WE'LL GET YOU OUT!"

It was Joe...

70

J ulie wasn't the only one the sea gave back that day. The other was Rolly Archer. Over two hundred miles south of Louisiana in the Gulf of Mexico, fate intervened on his behalf.

The ultra-deep drilling rig had automatic 'thruster' engines on the four corners of its floating platform. The thrusters kept the drill on station, in spite of the ocean currents. They were constantly in play, reacting to the GPS system that controlled them, moving the giant rig as necessary.

As the *Miranda* approached, propelled by the surface swells, the huge platform had responded to an ordinary GPS adjustment. The giant rig shifted just enough for the *Miranda* to scrape past.

Rolly was identified and taken to a Louisiana hospital. The Louisiana State Police announced that he would be returned to Key West in a day or two. As for *Miranda,* she was shipshape, requiring nothing but paint.

It seemed that Rolly knew seaworthy when he saw it.

71

It was the 28th of September, three days later, and Julie sat out on the pool patio at Twelve Gulf Wind Drive across the table from Rolly and Joe. David had prepared a sumptuous "welcome home" breakfast for Rolly to celebrate his safe return. As for her and Joe, they were headed back to Orlando around noon.

It was a perfect day, and Julie was admiring the yacht anchored in the canal. It looked pristine in the sun, at least on the side facing David's house. It rocked ever so gently now, in sharp contrast to a few days ago.

Julie reflected on the power and the mystery of the sea. It had provided her with an escape and hidden her from a killer.

Julie realized now that the sea had saved her before…all those years ago on Castle Cay. It had been impulsive and foolhardy to dive into that deadly current after Dan, and Julie had barely managed to get herself out of it. But when the adrenalin subsided and her own strength was gone, it was the breakers that held her up and deposited her on the shore.

The other side of the coin.

She sipped her orange juice and glanced over at Joe. He was chatting with Rolly. It struck her how handsome the two men were. Joe was taller, a little more muscular. Julie felt a warm glow in places the sun didn't reach.

David had gotten up...*again*...to see if the newspaper had been delivered.

"I just *hate* it when I can't read the paper with my coffee in the morning!" he had said, on the way to the front door. "Oh, good...it's here, everyone!" David called from inside the house.

Joe shook his head at David's theatrics and smiled at Julie.

David brought the paper out on the patio, and they each helped themselves to their favorite section.

"Anyone else want more coffee?"

"Yes, please," said Joe.

"Thank you, my dear," said David. "I'll have some more, too."

Julie refilled their cups, and then picked up the front section. There was a headline on page two that read, *"DRUG RING BUSTED IN BOSTON"*.

"Hey! Listen to *this*, you guys..."

She began to read:

"The Federal Bureau of Investigation, Boston Field Office, has just released information on a stunning, multiple-location drug bust carried out on Tuesday, September 25th. The late night raids resulted in the disruption of a major drug pipeline into the Massachusetts area, particularly in the city of Boston. Although there were simultaneous raids in Southern California and Utah, by far the biggest prize in this long-term investigation was taking down the distribution conspiracy in Boston and its suburbs. In this area alone, the Massachusetts State Police and the FBI arrested 32 individuals, and 18 separate search warrants were executed."

"U.S. Attorney Campbell Burns said, 'The Boston area has been plagued with this deadly drug ring for several years. This successful operation is the joint result of the cooperation between the Drug Enforcement Administration, the local and state police, and the FBI. We owe all of these men our gratitude, but we are especially grateful to FBI Special Agent Richard Lynch, who was killed in the line of duty. *Also, our wishes for a full recovery go out to FBI Special Agent Sherman Dixon, who was wounded in this operation.*'"

Joe's face fell as she read the last line.

"*Ah, no,*" he said. "Sherm wouldn't have gotten involved in this if it wasn't for me! I have to call him. Let me see that, please, Julie."

He took the paper from her, turned the page and

took over reading.

"It says the drug ring was 'orchestrated by the Tambini crime family' and that 'many of them were arrested, including Silvio Tambini and his son, Guido Tambini'. According to this, they recovered a big stash of 'drugs, firearms and cash', too. It says, 'the charges, if upheld, can carry anywhere from ten years to life in prison'."

Joe paused, scanning for more information.

"Shit...listen to this," he said.

"All the federal grand jury indictments were served, *except* for one related to money laundering, which charged Avram Solomon, a Boston businessman, under RICO, the 'Racketeer Influenced and Corrupt Organizations Act'."

"Except? What does that mean?"

"It means they didn't find him, Merlin. It means he got away."

72

"O w-w!"

Joe heard the howl through the cell phone. "What is it, Sherm?" You okay?"

"Yeah. It's my nurse, Jenna. She's killing me, pulling this damn dressing off my leg."

Joe could almost see the scene in Sherm's room at the Mass General Hospital. He could imagine the look of incredulous surprise on the nurse's face when she realized that the giant in the bed was actually a big baby.

When it came to Sherman, stoicism hadn't come with size. Joe flashed-back on their football years and had to cover the phone to muffle his laughter.

Their conversation turned serious again as soon as the nurse left the room. Sherman finished telling Joe about the raid on the drug lab in Waltham.

"I never saw so much blood come from one guy, Joe. I was right behind him. He got one in the neck and the blood was just *pumping* out...

"Anyhow, Next thing I knew I was in the back of

an ambulance.

"My Kevlar vest took two hits...bruised the hell out of my chest...but I'm not complaining about *that*. Thank the Lord for it! It was the one that went through my thigh that landed me in the hospital. It nicked an artery, and I lost a lot of blood. It's getting better, though. I'm doing good."

"Have you talked to Sondra and the girls?"

"Yeah. I told them not to bother coming up here. I'm going home tomorrow."

"That's great news. Hey, look, buddy. I'm sorry I got you mixed up in all this...sorry you got hurt."

"Joe. Forget it. It's my job. And being in on that bust is going to look real good in my file."

"All right, man, as long as you're okay. Thanks for everything you did, Sherm. I'm glad you're going home. Julie and I are headed home today, too."

"I read what happened down there in Key West, with that Susan Dwyer. How's Julie doing?"

"Julie's great, Sherm. She's an amazing woman, stronger now than she was before. She's made her peace with Marc Solomon's death," said Joe, "although we were both disappointed to hear that Avram Solomon slipped through the net up there."

"Yeah, you and a lot of other people, including me," said Sherm. "The guy just vanished. No cars were missing, so he must have left the dealership on foot. They checked all the cabs, the airlines, nothing. You can't pull off something like that without planning, Joe. That bastard was ready."

73

"Sherm's okay," said Joe, as they boarded the commuter plane to Orlando. "He was lucky; his vest stopped two bullets! Another one nicked a leg artery, but he's going to be fine. They're letting him go home tomorrow."

"That's great."

On the short flight home, Joe told Julie about his long friendship with Sherman. For the first time outside of an AA meeting, he talked about how they had *both* planned to join the Bureau...and how he had messed it up with alcohol.

And Julie, in turn, finally told him all about Dan.

Later, they shared a lingering kiss in Joe's car outside of Julie's condo.

"What next, Merlin?"

"A cover story for Luz and Janet?" she said, stepping out of the car.

Julie watched Joe pull away from the curb, knowing a new chapter in her life had opened. She turned, pulling her carry-on bag behind her, entered her building and went up to her condo.

Everything was as she had left it…and yet it wasn't. Marc was gone, but Julie felt reconnected to her past and she looked forward to the future. She opened the glass doors to the balcony. The outside air filled the living-room, cool and refreshing. Lake Eola sparkled in the sunshine and the squirrels scampered through the trees.

And then Sol nearly knocked her off the balcony, leaping onto the table.

Julie had momentarily felt like Dorothy, back from Oz.

But Sol sure as hell wasn't Toto.

EPILOGUE

"**W**ay to go, Merlin!"

Joe was right again. There were no ghosts on Castle Cay. Julie felt nothing but exhilaration as she reached the top of the ridge. The view of the island, the sea and the ocean liner was spectacular.

She was glad the ship on the horizon wouldn't be stopping there. Matt Castle had kept his family's island and built a private resort on it.

Julie thought wistfully of Dan O'Hara and Marc Solomon...especially Marc. It was almost a year since Marc's murder; a year of inevitabilities, some good things and some surprises.

It's been said that when one door closes, another opens. When Solomon Chrysler closed its doors, Pete and Joan Soldano bought the Lynn store.

Julie smiled, glad for her two friends.

Her thoughts turned to Tom Connor, Marc's father. Matt Castle had seen to it that his friend and law partner was given all of his son's paintings. Tom, in gratitude, had given one each to Julie and Joe, and had chosen for the rest to remain as a permanent exhibit in the expanded Sandpiper Art Gallery in Key West, managed by David Harris.

The best news of all, however, had come just two weeks ago, when they located Avram Solomon, in spite of his new identity. It was all over the news…

It happened during Silvio Tambini's trial. One of the state's witnesses, a certain William Bonafacci, also known as "Billy Bones," was testifying about the order of events leading up to Silvio Tambini's decision to move the drug lab out of the Waltham warehouse owned by Solomon Chrysler.

"So, Mr. Bonafacci, please tell us, in your own words, exactly what triggered this decision to 'clear out' of Waltham."

"Well, see, we was watchin' the car…"

"And what car was that?"

"It was a gray Sebring sedan…you know, a new one…on the storage lot. We seen Avram Solomon drive it there and put this bag in the trunk. So we popped it."

"You 'popped it'. Do you mean you opened the trunk?"

"Yeah."

"And what was in the bag?"

"Money, papers. A passport and stuff."

"And did you report this to Silvio Tambini?"

"Of course!"

"*All right, Mr. Bonafacci. You mentioned that there was 'a passport' in the bag. Did you see the picture on the passport?*"

"*Yeah, it was Avram Solomon.*"

"*For the record, Mr. Bonafacci, do you remember the name on the passport?*"

"*No. But it wasn't Houdini...he didn't get out of the trunk!*"

Chuckling, Julie closed her eyes and turned her face up to the sun.

TURN THE PAGE
FOR A PREVIEW OF

Swan
Song

JULIE O'HARA
MYSTERY SERIES,
BOOK TWO

LEE HANSON

Swan Song

A Julie O'Hara Novel

PROLOGUE

He had to know if her car was still there.

It was almost five in the morning and still dark. He sat in the SUV, parked at the edge of Lake Eola Park in Orlando, staring at the Lexus. How many hours had he spent watching her house, her office, her car? He didn't know. It didn't matter.

He was going to make her pay.

His body felt stiff like a discarded, lifeless marionette. He jerked the door open and got out, sucking down a lungful of cool, moist air. To his great surprise, he saw her tall figure headed toward him. Her head was down and she was striding purposefully up East Robinson.

Quick! Get the knife!

He popped open the glove compartment and grabbed it.

A black chain-link fence prevented access to the foliage in front of the Lexus, so he simply dropped down below the front of the car, out of sight.

She stood next to the car, a thin strap across her body. She pulled the flat Louis Vuitton purse around to the front, but she never got the little bag unzipped. He grabbed her around the neck from behind, flashing the knife in her face.

She yelped in fear, and he lifted her chin with the flat side of the blade.

"Shut up or I'll cut you!"

He dragged her past the fence, over the grass toward the SUV.

Her terror doubled as she realized she was about to be forced into a car. When he loosened his grip for a moment, she wrenched herself free and saw his face.

"You?!"

She bolted and ran down the three or four steps leading through the trees toward the lake. A few feet behind her, he managed to grab her sweater and yanked it, pulling her into the cover of the trees. Out of control and as panicked as she was, he swiped the knife wildly at her, right and left.

"Ahh!" She cried out, as the blade sliced downward on her wrist.

Hugging her cut right hand tight to her body, she swung her left arm at him with all her might, connecting solidly with his right forearm, knocking the knife from his hand.

For a heartbeat or two, he looked at his empty hand. She seized the moment…and the knife.

She lunged at him, and he jumped back.

"Bitch! I'm going to kill you!"

Desperate to get away from him, she shot a look over her shoulder and quickly backed onto the nearby walkway that circled the lake. A dense fog hung over the water and widely spaced lanterns created dim pearls of light strung along the concrete.

Swinging the knife back and forth, she continued to hold him at bay, feeling weaker by the minute. Her wrist was throbbing. She pulled it away from her chest and looked down. Her blood was pumping out in spurts. Horrified, she pressed it tightly to her body again, looking frantically up and down the walkway for someone…*anyone* who could help her!

There was no one.

She turned and ran, lifting legs that felt like lead.

The swan boats! They were directly ahead! She ran past the outdoor tables of a darkened restaurant, and veered into a small grouping of trees at the entrance to the boat dock. There was a knee-high, black gate with a loose cable securing it. She pushed it down with the knife, stepped through and staggered to the end of the short dock.

He was right on her heels!

She whirled and lunged at him again, and he backed up to the gate.

Pain etching her face, she threatened him with the knife as she fumbled with her injured hand, finally unhooking the furthest swan boat. She threw the knife in and fell in behind it. He made a grab for the boat, but his hand slipped as she gathered the last of her strength and pushed down hard on the pedals.

The swan slid away, rippling the still, smoked glass surface of the lake. She wasn't more than a few feet out when she lost consciousness. Adrift, the silvery swan and its passenger slipped into a shroud of fog.

1

January 28, 2010

Julie O'Hara opened her eyes, nose to nose with Sol, her Bengal cat, who sounded like a trolling motorboat and weighed nearly as much. He was wearing his usual expression of feline content.

She pushed him away, glancing at the eerie, neon-green numbers on her alarm clock...*6:00*. She pulled the comforter over her head, trying to ignore both the clock and the cat. But it was no use. A busy day loomed in front of her.

Julie was a body language expert known professionally by the single name, "Merlin". In addition to her consulting and corporate training, she was currently in the process of writing a book. Her manuscript, *Clues, A Body Language Guide*, was undergoing a rewrite. Reorganizing *Clues* along the lines suggested by her editor would strengthen the book, and Julie had committed her mornings to the task. Later, she had a consulting appointment with John Tate, an attorney, to assist him with jury selection for an upcoming trial.

That will probably take all afternoon. I better get going.

Sighing, she pushed the cat and the cover aside and swung her long legs over the side of the bed. Clad in an oversized gray cotton tee-shirt, she opened the French door to the balcony and stepped outside into the half-light, hugging herself against the cool January air that raised goose bumps on her bare arms and legs.

Julie looked out over Lake Eola Park from her fourth-floor condo. She could just make out the top of the lake's signature fountain, lights out and still, sitting in the center of the twenty-three acre Downtown lake. It appeared to be floating on a thick blanket of fog which clung to the surface of the water. Beyond the lake and its walkway, the trees were softly defined mounds of dusky green, foothills at the base of the cityscape. Julie smiled, noting that the fog had retreated from the lantern-studded sidewalk.

She went back inside and flicked on the light. She pulled on a pair of jeans and a sweatshirt and gathered her wild hair up into a ponytail. A quick glance in the mirror caused her to do a double-take. Her hairdresser had recently added quite a bit of red to her hair, and she wasn't sure how she felt about that yet.

Sol growled softly and rubbed against her legs, threatening to trip her as she walked into the kitchen. His food and water dishes were empty. Julie filled them and stroked the cat affectionately while he lapped the fresh water.

Bending, she tied her running shoes on, and grabbed her keys and her new cell phone. Julie still marveled at how such a small, flat thing could give her internet access and directions and everything else. She shoved it into a handy watch-pocket in her jeans.

"Back in a jiffy, Handsome," she said to the cat, whose face was now buried in his dry food dish.

For a second, Julie contemplated taking the stairs to the ground level, but, chiding herself, she opted for the elevator instead. Outside, not a soul was in sight. Her building was mostly asleep, with just the odd apartment, here and there, winking a light. The moon was a faint crescent in the half-dark sky, the stars invisible, awaiting the sunrise.

A lone car passed in front of her as she crossed Central and trotted down the broad steps to the wide walkway that circled the lake.

She started an easy, loping run, but the cool air was wonderful, and soon, exhilarated, she was running flat-out. Three-quarters of the way around the lake, near the dock and the swan boats, she had to stop and catch her breath.

She stood there, head down, hands on her hips, huffing and puffing. At last, her breathing slowed and she straightened up, facing the water.

An odd, irregular tapping sound out on the lake had caught her attention.

The sun was just peeking through the city buildings on the eastern side of the urban park, and the long shadows of the trees still covered the walkway and part of the water like dappled gray gauze. As Julie peered through the dissipating fog, she saw that it was one of the paddleboats that must have come loose and drifted to the center of the lake. She could see the silvery-white swan boat bobbing up and down, bumping into the fountain, the sound carrying on the still air.

There was something in the boat.

Julie squinted, focusing as the sky grew lighter.

There was something trailing in the water…

Dawn broke over Lake Eola and Julie about the same time.

That's a woman's ARM.

Stunned, she pulled out her cell phone and called 911.

The police would be there "shortly". Julie was to "stay at the scene". That was fine with her. Suddenly, her busy day had lost all importance. She had no desire to leave the park before the poor woman in the boat.

Two Orlando Park Service employees were pedaling toward her on their city bicycles. She waved both arms at them to stop.

"Hey!" she said, pointing toward the fountain. "There's a woman in that loose swan boat out there!"

"What?"

"Look!" she said, pointing again. "I'm sure it's a woman. I've already called the police. They should be here any minute."

Their bikes fell to the ground as they hurried out on the dock, stepping over the low, partially opened gate.

"Christ, Hal. It *is* a woman!" said the first one.

He pulled out his cell phone.

Julie was standing before the gate at the entrance to the dock listening to the urgent, one-sided conversation. There was some kind of loose cable, like a big bike lock, looped through the two short, swinging sections of the little gate. It was stretched wide, near the ground.

Anyone could just step through here.

They rejoined Julie and asked her when she first noticed the boat. She explained that she couldn't see that side of the fountain from where she'd started her run, and besides, it was too foggy out on the lake. She told them that she'd just seen the loose swan boat when the sun came up, right before she flagged them down. They asked her if she'd seen anyone else, and she told them she hadn't seen another soul.

It wasn't long before the three of them had morphed into a horde: Police, Emergency Techs, a CSI unit, more Park Service people and paparazzi. The same questions were asked of her and answered over and over again.

The police had blocked off the walkway and all the landscaped area near it, isolating the whole northwest corner of the park bordered by Rosalind Avenue and East Robinson up to Eola Parkway. Patrol cars, emergency vehicles and TV trucks lined the curbs. Outside of the police cordon, condo dwellers began to appear on their lakeside balconies, while other curious onlookers gathered in groups on the walkway, abuzz with speculation. Motorists in the vicinity craned their necks and slowed to a crawl, creating a traffic jam that spread like lava.

The crowd on the dock finally parted and Julie could see the Disney Amphitheatre in the background. At last she got a glimpse of the young woman as they carefully lifted her from the swan boat. A light blue sweater stained with blood. Her long neck hung back loosely and her hair was short and dark, ebony against pale skin.

Snow White in a fractured fairytale...

Lee Hanson, a Boston native and Florida transplant, is the author of The Julie O'Hara Mystery Series, including *Castle Cay, Swan Song* and *Mystral Murder.* Her novels, featuring body language expert, Julie O'Hara, have been called "the answer to a mystery addict's prayer", a line that makes the author smile...and keeps her writing.

Made in the USA
Middletown, DE
22 October 2015